"It makes sense why you wouldn't want to get involved with the customers."

"That doesn't have anything to do with it. I just like to keep my distance in general." Alex sure wasn't proving the truth of that statement, because as he said the words, he noticed that he'd somehow managed to scoot his sleeping bag closer to hers. "I like my life the way it is."

"Of course you do," she said, that sexy soft whisper back.

Another clap of thunder shuddered through the trees outside, and he found himself grasping the edge of her sleeping bag, tugging it toward him. He heard Charlotte's indrawn breath. But she didn't pull away.

"You live in your world and I live in mine," he said, talking more to himself, wanting reassurance that despite their physical proximity, he still had some emotional boundaries left.

Their faces were inches apart. "You said it yourself, Alex. What happens out here stays out here."

But what exactly was happening? He could navigate the wild mountain terrain in the snow without a GPS, but he'd never trusted himself to read women very well unless they provided him with a clear course.

"Are you sure about this?" he asked, not wanting to question what exactly this was.

A FAMILY UNDER
THE STARS

BY
CHRISTY JEFFRIES

First Published in Great Britain 2017
By Mills & Boon, an imprint of HarperCollins*Publishers*
1 London Bridge Street, London, SE1 9GF

© 2017 Christy Jeffries

ISBN: 978-0-263-92284-4

23-0317

Our policy is to use papers that are natural, renewable and recyclable products and made from wood grown in sustainable forests. The logging and manufacturing processes conform to the legal environmental regulations of the country of origin.

Printed and bound in Spain
by CPI, Barcelona

Christy Jeffries graduated from the University of California, Irvine, with a degree in criminology and received her Juris Doctor from California Western School of Law. But drafting court documents and working in law enforcement was merely an apprenticeship for her current career in the dynamic field of mummyhood and romance writing. She lives in Southern California with her patient husband, two energetic sons and one sassy grandmother. Follow her online at www.christyjeffries.com.

To my happy little camper.
Whether it's collecting pine cones, helping Daddy set up the tent or roasting marshmallows over the fire (despite the fact that you only eat the chocolate out of your s'mores), your enthusiasm for the great outdoors is immeasurable and so much fun to witness. I can't wait for our next camping adventure. I love you, Peanut.

Chapter One

Alex Russell glanced over his shoulder at the silver four-door Jeep pulling up behind him, its color matching the clouds overhead, which in turn matched his mood. The decals plastered to the side of the vehicle were a brighter version of the ones stenciled on the raft he was stocking with dry boxes, paddles and waterproof bags.

His grandfather, who everyone in western Idaho—including Alex—referred to as Commodore due to the man's expertise in navigating the Sugar River, hopped out of the driver's side while the female passenger remained inside talking on her cell phone. Alex rolled his eyes. Exactly the kind of city slicker he'd figured.

But when Alex's father called him this morning, hacking up a lung and complaining about a sore throat, Alex had immediately offered to take over as the guide for today's whitewater excursion. While his dad could probably steer through these rapids blindfolded, let alone with a fever of 103, it wouldn't be good for business to get the paying customers sick. It was bad enough that they had to expose the public to Commodore's ever-present crotchetiness, but they really needed someone to run the shuttle between the put-in and pickup locations.

"I thought Dad said there were supposed to be five in the group today," Alex said when his grandfather approached.

"S'posed to be." Commodore had never been described as a people person and always kept a toothpick clamped tightly between his teeth, probably as an excuse to avoid talking. It gave his weathered face a permanent grimace, like Popeye smoking his pipe, and it gave Alex a permanent headache trying to communicate with the seventy-five-year-old man.

"So, what happened to everyone else?"

"Don't know." Commodore limped over to the raft, checked the carabineers and tested out the tautness on the slings harnessed near the stern. "Some of us mind our own business."

Alex took off his polarized sunglasses, letting them dangle from the strap around his neck, and rubbed the bridge of his nose. He was tempted to remind his grandfather that this *was* their business, their family's bread and butter. But that would only serve as an invitation to launch into another round of the ongoing argument about why Commodore was no longer allowed to do the bookkeeping for Russell's Sports. "You gotta give me more info than that, Com."

Com jerked the remaining half of his right thumb at

the Jeep. "Gal's name is Charlotte Folsom. Bankroller, far as I can tell. You want more than that, you can ask her yourself when she gets off the phone."

Bankroller was the term some people in their small town of Sugar Falls, Idaho, used to refer to the tourists who vacationed on the mountain and, in the course of a weekend, injected plenty of their big-city dollars into the local economy. It probably wasn't the politest thing to call the patrons that kept their small family company afloat, but Commodore wasn't exactly known for his civility or his business acumen.

Alex looked at his watch. How long was her call going to take? He was surprised the woman even had reception this far upriver. "Is she allergic to the fresh air or something?"

"Not that she mentioned when she signed the release form." His grandfather snorted before the last part, confirming that the old man was still miffed that his son and grandson had taken over the legal side of the business.

"Then why isn't she getting out of the car?"

Yet, as soon as Alex asked the question, the woman opened the Jeep door. He noticed her hair first because it was the exact shade of his favorite dark chocolate–covered granola bar. It was styled as plainly and conservatively as possible, stick straight and cut in a uniform line just below her shoulders, with a headband holding everything but the thick sweeping bangs away from her face.

And what a face it was. Her cheekbones were high and sharp, her nose elegant and straight, and her lips reminded him of the cotton candy his dad bought him the first time they'd attended a minor league baseball game. They were pink and full and caused a spike in his bloodstream, like an instant sugar rush.

Man, something about this lady kept making him think of food.

"Hello," she said, reaching out her hand. "I'm Charlotte Folsom. I'm terribly sorry for being on the phone when we arrived, but my editor had an update on my crew's flight."

"Your crew?" Alex asked, shifting his attention to the long, pale fingers clasped inside his. The ones that looked much too delicate to handle an oar.

"Yes. The producer, her assistant and the two photographers. They were supposed to fly into Spokane, but were diverted to Seattle because of a lightning storm. I don't think they're going to make it." She looked up at the gray sky. "It's not a problem, is it?"

"The weather or the lack of people?"

"Either."

"Nah. Weather's fine." Commodore shifted his toothpick to the right side of his mouth. "And Miss Folsom's rowed before, so you should be good to go."

Alex's untraditional upbringing meant that he'd learned to steer a raft before he'd learned to a drive a car. So he wasn't concerned about his own ability to handle the river singlehandedly, but he would prefer having someone aboard who knew what they were doing. Unfortunately, every visiting tourist had a different definition of what constituted experience, and paddling through Class IV rapids required a lot more skill than most novices realized.

Not that he wanted to jump to any unfair conclusions about Charlotte Folsom, but Alex had been in business with his family long enough to recognize a greenhorn trying too hard to look the part. He wouldn't be surprised if she'd just cut the price tags off her athletic clothes this morning.

"How many times have you been whitewater rafting?" he asked, setting his sunglasses back over his eyes so he didn't offend the woman with an inadvertent look of doubt.

"Oh, this is my first time rafting. But when I was in middle school, my bunk won the canoeing finals two years in a row at Camp Butterhorn."

Commodore whistled around his toothpick as if this was some sort of accomplishment. Were they serious? Com knew better than anyone else that rowing a canoe at some fancy sleepaway camp in seventh grade was *not* the same thing as navigating a six-man raft down the roaring Sugar River. Actually, Alex was just assuming the camp had been a fancy one judging by the rock-sized diamond studs in Miss Folsom's ears and the way she stood tall and poised in her overpriced, brand-new skin-tight paddling pants and bright pink, waterproof North Face jacket.

His eyes shot down to her left hand, noting the absence of a wedding ring on her finger. Not that he was interested in her marital status. Alex preferred his women a lot less frilly and way more down-to-earth. And the one standing before him, who'd given off that supermodel vibe even before she'd mentioned having a camera crew, looked more suitable to being on the cover of the Neiman Marcus holiday book than an REI catalog. He simply didn't want anyone losing any valuable jewelry on his watch.

"Here's that lip cream I was telling you about in the car, Mr.... I mean Commodore." Her quick correction indicated that Com had already warned her that he only answered to the nickname. Then she reached into a small pack slung over her shoulder and pulled out a jar of something. "This will really help with the dryness and the cracks. I told you I never leave home without it. Just put it on like this..."

She dipped a finger inside the tiny glass container and then proceeded to spread some sort of balm all over her own lips. Alex sucked in his breath when she held out the open container to his grandfather. He waited for the old guy—who'd once walked out in the middle of a haircut when the new barber offered to apply a deep conditioning treatment—to let out a string of curses about beauty product nonsense. But Com scrunched his eyes into slits as he swiped his stubby fingers across his tightly clamped frown, reminding Alex of one of the kids he coached in Pop Warner who'd accepted his teammates' dare to eat a spoonful of spicy red peppers at the after-game pizza party.

"Actually, maybe we should just reschedule this whole thing," Alex offered and saw his grandfather's squint deepen and the barely perceptible shake of the elder Russell's silver crew-cut head. He wasn't sure if Com's reaction was to Alex's suggestion or to the novelty of having a foreign—and probably highly expensive—substance applied to any part of his anatomy.

"We can't reschedule," she said a bit forcefully, and Alex had the sense that not many people said "no" to Charlotte Folsom. "My magazine is on a deadline. We were already rushing to get the article done last week, but then I had child care issues and one of our columnists came down with a horrendous case of food poisoning so we had to scrap his review of Indonesian food trucks. So if I can't come up with at least a few shots and five thousand words on gourmet dining off the land, then next month's issue will completely tank."

Child care issues? So the woman had kids, but no wedding ring? Not that it was any of Alex's business, he told himself as he rocked back on his heels. He didn't mind making small talk with the customers, but he rarely found himself curious about anything beyond their skill level and whether he'd need to keep them from getting killed while participating in an extreme sport they shouldn't be doing in the first place. It was only the unusualness of the situation that had him wondering why a lady as beautiful as Charlotte Folsom was single. In his experience, it usually meant that the woman was too much of a pain for any man to deal with.

Again, not his business. What *was* his business was Russell's Sports and how to turn a better profit this year. Thanks to Commodore's refusal to book a corporate retreat last year and some bad online reviews of his grandfather's customer service, the company's savings account was at an all-time low.

Last week, his father had mentioned something about a San Francisco–based magazine booking them for some sort of photo shoot. Having no interest in any publication that didn't contain ads for Bass Pro Shops or Cabela's, Alex had just chalked the whole thing up to some travel article that might garner them some free publicity. Suddenly, this was sounding like more than he'd bargained for.

"Wait, back up." He ran a hand over his face, his palm scratching against the dark-brown stubble on his chin. "What's the point of going through all the effort of staging a photo shoot if the model is the only person who showed up?"

Miss Folsom slid her oversized tortoiseshell sunglasses off and Alex found himself looking into eyes that weren't quite purple, but weren't quite blue. "I'm not the model. The *food* is the model."

"What food?" Alex looked back at his grandfather, shrugged as if to say, *not my problem*, then turned and walked over to the Jeep, presumably to grab more gear out of the back.

"Mr. Russell, I work for *Fine Tastes*. It's one of the top cooking and home entertainment magazines in the industry. I thought our producer had explained that we're doing a feature article on glamping and resourcing foods indigenous to the wilderness areas in order to create gourmet al fresco meals."

"What the hell is glamping?" Commodore called out from behind the tailgate before Alex could ask what al fresco meant.

"It's glamorous camping," she said, then beamed a wide smile at his grandfather. "I know it's an oxymoron, but it's all the rage right now with urban families."

"Sounds moronic, all right," Commodore said, carrying over a bright orange bag then rubbing his lips together. It was tough to tell with the bobbing toothpick, but it almost seemed as though the old guy wasn't quite frowning. Maybe that lip balm contained some magical ingredient that cured personality disorders.

The woman laughed, a throaty sound that was both way too feminine and way more genuine than he'd expected, and Alex stared at his grandfather, trying to determine what it was this particular lady had done to make the cantankerous Commodore Russell fall so completely under her spell.

He tried to stop his judgmental thoughts, reminding himself that not every woman from an overpopulated metropolis was his mother. Nor did many women take the time to pick a few fallen pine needles off his grandfather's flannel shirt as the man passed by.

Alex asked, "So, what exactly is the goal for this two-day excursion if you don't have your crew to help with the article?"

Because he was only supposed to be here as a guide. He certainly wasn't going to glamp it up with her or otherwise assist in—what did she call it? Resourcing indigenous foods? Sure, she seemed sweet enough toward Com, but Alex could already see her as the type to start ordering him around, treating him as some sort of low-level assistant who was there to do the job of her entire crew.

"Frankly," she said, turning that wide smile on him, "since time and weather are already a potential issue, I don't see the need to make this a two-day excursion. We can just make a few stops along the river and stage a couple of scenes for the pictures. Then, if you don't mind me conducting an informal interview of sorts, I can pick your brain and get a good enough idea of what the experience would be like so I can convey that to our readers."

Alex looked up at the gray sky again. "Honestly, I don't even know if we have one day. What does your old knee say, Com?"

His grandfather reached down to pat his arthritic leg, which was usually a better weather forecaster than most barometer stations. "Should hold off until tonight."

"You sure?" Alex asked, noticing the subtle wobble of the toothpick.

"Sure as death and taxes."

"When was the last time *you* paid taxes?" Alex mumbled under his breath. It was now a running joke among family and friends that Commodore Russell wasn't always on the most hospitable terms with his neighbors *or* the IRS, which was why Alex and his dad kept the old man away from the financial side of the business, as well as many of the customers. Of course, that running joke was also the reason why they really couldn't afford to cancel this trip. The beginning of the season was right around the corner and Russell's Sports needed all the positive publicity it could get.

"If I'm wrong, then you get a lil' wet," Com said, a firm challenge in the man's clear green eyes. It was no secret that Alex inherited his tan coloring and his competitive athletic spirit from the paternal side of the family. As well as his dry lips, apparently. He pulled out his plain store-bought lip balm and swiped it on, wishing the familiar gesture would sooth his apprehension, as well.

"Please, Mr. Russell," Miss Folsom said, her eyes taking on a darker, more serious hue. "Just for a couple of hours. I know it'll be more of a challenge for you than for me, but I have a friend watching my daughters back in town. I had to pull them out of school and make all kinds of alternate travel arrangements so I could make this article work. Plus, I told them Mommy was going to bring them back a wilderness treasure and I would hate to disappoint them."

He had no clue what a wilderness treasure was, but Alex was a sucker for a challenge. And for kids. It was why he volunteered as a coach for almost every recreational league in town and ran a youth day camp during the summers. He was also a team player when it came to the family business and didn't want to let his dad down.

So, against his better judgment, he decided not to disappoint anyone. "Let's get the rest of your gear. I'll explain the basics to you while we load up."

They were only two miles downriver and Charlotte wished she hadn't convinced herself, let alone her stoic rafting guide, that this was a good idea. What Charlotte hadn't told the Russell men was that she desperately needed this article to help launch her career to the next level by—hopefully—winning a shot as a permanent contributor for a nationally syndicated cooking show. Sure, doing freelance writing for *Fine Tastes* had been a blessing after Mitchell had gone to prison, leaving her to raise their two daughters alone. But after some of the webisodes on her personal blog started gaining upward of 400,000 hits per day, her editor and several local news channels back in San Francisco were now referring to her as a younger, fresher Martha Stewart, and if Charlotte could turn her home and lifestyle brand into a success, then she'd finally be able to prove to her parents and her ex-husband that she was more than something to be paraded about at cocktail parties and charity events.

"Let's pull out here," Alex Russell finally said from his higher perch on the raft behind her.

Thank God. Charlotte had been under the impression that she was in decent shape since she did Pilates regularly and ran for thirty minutes on her home tread-mill every day. But her upper arms felt like they were on fire after only an hour of paddling.

The boat was too big for just the two of them, but they needed the extra supplies she'd already packed to make the photos look more legitimate. Initially, she'd thought it would be easier and quicker to just take off in the inflatable raft with the well-muscled outdoorsman who gave new meaning to the phrase *ruggedly hand-some* and whose masculine appearance reminded her that when she'd divorced her husband two years ago, she hadn't divorced her libido. But even if she put her physical reaction to Alex Russell's looks aside—which she could easily do—there were other complications to being out in the middle of nowhere, cut off from ev-erything she was used to.

Charlotte had never left her children alone over-night, and although her friend Kylie had offered to host the girls for their first-ever slumber party back in the town of Sugar Falls, Charlotte was relieved they'd be cutting this two-day excursion short. Not that she didn't appreciate the natural beauty around her—or the one in the boat with her—she just didn't feel com-fortable being out of communication with her daugh-ters in case something happened to them. Or in case they needed her.

Kylie had laughed at the fact that Charlotte arrived in town last night with eight suitcases, half of the stuff belonging to her daughters. But she didn't want them to be without their favorite blankets, stuffed animals, markers, pajamas—long sleeved for cooler weather and shorts if it became too warm—Junie B. Jones books or unicorn puzzles.

It would've just been smarter to postpone the whole weekend. Or call it off. The colorful Victorian buildings in the quaint mountain town where her friend lived housed plenty of antiques shops and homey restaurants that could have filled the pages of her magazine with food and decorating ideas.

But then her article wouldn't have been much more interesting than a destination travel piece, and the career she'd been trying to build would never gain traction.

Plus, she'd recently read an autobiography by a woman who, years ago, had left her life as a political speechwriter to travel to Idaho to commune with nature and find herself. The book opened Charlotte's eyes to how people could learn to adapt with the barest of necessities and find beauty all around them.

But clearly, that author had lived a more unfettered life than Charlotte, who'd had to decide whether to leave behind her kids. Charlotte had debated whether or not to go during most of the ride to the site, and then again for several minutes before they'd finally launched the raft and waved goodbye to the senior Russell, an interesting character who liked putting on a show of being ornery and gruff.

Now, though, her decision had been made. She was out here on this beautiful river, which was way more choppy and rock-filled than she'd expected, and she would make the best out of the situation.

Even if her arms turned to al dente linguini from rowing so much. This was nothing like sleepaway camp, and she'd bet the river jock sitting behind her had struggled to keep a straight face when she'd stupidly boasted about her experience.

"Can I give you a hand with that?" she asked the younger Russell when he hopped out of the raft and waded through the knee-deep water to pull the raft toward the pebbly shore. She may not be much in the paddling department, but she was used to doing everything for herself and for her girls back home. Charlotte hated being taken care of, or worse—having someone *think* she needed to be taken care of.

"Nope. You're the customer." The man's sleeves were rolled above his forearms and she tried not to stare at the defined muscles as he easily maneuvered the whole thing, including her and the heavy supplies, close to a sturdy-looking overgrown bush submerged in the water.

Besides some initial instructions and an overview of the local terrain and hidden dangers lurking beneath the river's surface, her guide hadn't been too talkative up until this point. And Charlotte had been concentrating so hard on her paddling—and not plowing them into a submerged boulder—that she hadn't asked many questions. In fact, her clenched jaw was almost as sore as her arms.

"You don't have to treat me as a customer," she said, trying to gracefully climb out of the raft while he secured the rope tie to one of the thicker branches. "I know the circumstances are not ideal and I'd like to pull my own weight."

"Miss Folsom," he started, but she quickly interrupted him.

"Please, call me Charlotte. Being called Miss Folsom reminds me of when I was in boarding school and would get called to the headmistress's office."

He took off his sunglasses and let his smoky green eyes travel up and down the length of her body before saying, "You don't really strike me as the type to get into trouble."

Really? Because she sure felt like she was in trouble just by the way his tone had seemed to grow in exasperation as the afternoon wore on. Charlotte unbuckled her life vest, thinking it had suddenly grown too tight. "I'm not."

"In my experience—" he walked to the rear of the raft and unstrapped one of the boxes of supplies his grandfather had tied down before driving off and leaving them all alone "—when people go to the principal's office, it's because their teachers can't handle them."

"Well, in my case, it was typically because my parents were too busy to handle me. No, not like that," she said quickly when she realized that sounded even worse. "I didn't need handling. I was usually called into the office to find out that I'd be staying on campus during holiday breaks."

"Your parents still around?" he asked. She would've thought his thick baritone voice sounded a bit annoyed if he'd lifted his head out of the open supply crate long enough to look in her direction.

"Well, they're alive, if that's what you mean. Mother is in Paris, and the last time I spoke with her assistant, she said my father was in Dubai on business."

Mr. Russell, who'd yet to return the courtesy of inviting her to use his first name, raised his head, and Charlotte immediately recognized the sympathetic look in his eyes. She'd seen it all her life. Poor little rich girl, abandoned and unloved. Poor little Charlotte, who had to go home with the school employees for Christmas vacation because her parents were vacationing out of the country. Poor little Charlotte, who was so desperate for love and acceptance, she married the first guy who showed a speck of interest in her and ended up betrayed, bankrupt and on the cover of every newspaper in Northern California when her ex-husband was sentenced to ninety-eight years for wire fraud, money laundering and various investment schemes.

"Actually," she continued, before he could make one of those pitying comments or pretend to feel sorry for her, "it ended up working out to my benefit. Normally, students weren't allowed in the dining hall after meals, but Mrs. Jackson—she was the head chef—decided I made an eager pupil. My love of cooking started there and I wouldn't trade the knowledge or the experience for anything."

Perhaps her smile was a bit too cheerful, because the handsome guide looked up at the clouds billowing overhead and must've decided she needed his sympathy anyway.

"My lunch lady was named Mrs. Snook and, trust me, nobody wanted to go into her kitchen after hours. So I hope you have something other than sloppy joes and tater tots planned for your staged photo shoot."

"I don't suppose you could catch us a fish real quick while I forage around for some fresh herbs and root vegetables?"

"Real quick, huh?"

"I would do it myself, but I've never been fishing before and I figured it would take you twice as long to have to teach me. Unless you'd rather do the foraging?"

"Nope," he said, the smirk on his lips much more tolerable than pity. "I absolutely do not want to do any foraging. What's wrong with just slapping a striped bass on the cast-iron skillet and calling it a day? Or, better yet, we could open one of the pouches of tuna we keep in the emergency kit."

She couldn't help but wrinkle her nose at the mention of canned fish. "Well, the whole point of the article is to demonstrate the ability to create a five-star dining experience in the wilderness. I know it's not the easiest route to take, but since the purpose of the photos is to make ordinary things look more desirable, I have to put a bit more effort into the presentation."

"Nothing wrong with ordinary things looking ordinary, either."

She wasn't sure she'd heard his grumbled words correctly. "What's that?"

"Nothing," he muttered. She'd noticed that he'd also slathered on sunscreen before they'd left and kept a green ball cap with the team name Comets pulled down low on his head. After seeing his grandfather's hard-earned, but sun-damaged skin, it was easy to see why Alex was more careful to protect his own.

Her guide pulled out a fishing pole that had been strapped inside the raft. "I'll catch a fish, but I'm not comfortable with you wandering far from the beach. Rule number one is stay within sight."

"I'll stick close by." The promise would be an easy one to keep. Charlotte wasn't a fan of being alone and she was even less a fan of being alone and lost in the wilds, no matter how breathtaking they were. She tilted her neck to take in the tall pines and rugged green landscape. "It's absolutely beautiful here. I might take a few pictures of the scenery."

"Just don't try and make it look too desirable," he said, as he tied a hook to the end of his line. "Last thing we need is a bunch of city folks wanting to come up and beautify the land."

Commodore—she still smiled when she thought of the older man introducing himself by a nickname she'd only ever associated with yachting—had made virtually the same plea on the drive to the put-in location. Like grandfather, like grandson. Of course, Charlotte could understand why the locals would want to keep their pristine rivers and mountains exactly the way they were. The views were amazingly spectacular. But the remote area also lacked all the modern conveniences of San Francisco.

She pulled her waterproof pack out of the raft and looked inside at the disposable box encased in a clear plastic shell. Commodore had said, in not so many words, that it had been left behind by one of their previous guests. This wasn't exactly what she'd had in mind when she'd asked for a waterproof camera, but she couldn't very well expect them to have professional photography equipment on hand just because her crew hadn't showed up with theirs.

Charlotte would get better quality shots from her cell phone, which was also in its own plastic case, bought specifically for this trip. She checked the signal, hoping for a text from Kylie saying the girls were okay and doing well. But there was still no reception. She'd left a message for them before they'd launched into the river, and Commodore said he knew the Gregsons and would personally stop by Kylie's house to make sure her friend got the message.

She took some shots of the river and the mountains in the distance, then studied the dark, damp soil for any clues as to what may be growing nearby. Good thing she'd studied up on the local plant life because the last thing she wanted to do was ask Mr. Preserve-the-Land for more help. She looked back to where he was balancing on a boulder, holding a fishing pole and far enough away that he couldn't hear her gasp of breath at his handsome profile and masculine stance.

This wasn't the type of scenery she'd originally envisioned when the magazine had booked her trip. And she would die of shame if he turned in that exact second and caught her snapping a photo of him. But how could she pass up the chance? The red plaid shirt couldn't hide his athletic build any better than the thick dark stubble on his jaw could hide his handsome looks. Alex Russell looked exactly like every woman's dream of a rugged mountain man come to life and Charlotte told herself it would've been sloppy journalism to not capture the alluring image.

She knew what her readers wanted, even if she was only providing the perception of an ideal setting with an ideal man. The key word was *perception*. Charlotte had absolutely no idea what kind of man Alex Russell was. And she knew from past experience that it would take more than a couple of hours on the Sugar River to find out that he probably wasn't anything like he seemed. Nobody ever was. She glanced down at the clock on her phone. Good thing she had a job to do and two loving daughters to hurry back to. She didn't have time for disillusionment today.

Chapter Two

"Here's the deal," her guide said less than ten minutes later, as he walked toward Charlotte with his fishing pole resting on one of his broad shoulders. She had to command the air to exhale from her lungs.

Alex glanced down at her dirt-creased fingers, the ones that had been digging up wild ginger roots in the fertile soil, and, embarrassed, Charlotte wiped them clean on her pants. "This rain isn't going to hold off for much longer. I know you'd prefer to make things look as realistic as possible, but I think it'd be safer for us to shove off and try to get a few more miles downriver before we do much more."

"What about the fish?" She swallowed, trying not to look directly into the bulging dead eyes of the trout he'd easily caught.

"We can cook it when we stop next. Back at the

put-in, I went over the map with my grandfather and gave him an itinerary of sorts, just in case things get dicey and someone needs to come looking for us."

Dicey? That didn't sound good. Blood rushed to her feet, giving Charlotte the urge to put these too-snug hiking boots in motion and run back to Sugar Falls. Her children had already lost one parent, so to speak, and Charlotte didn't believe in taking any unnecessary risks. She flexed her toes, telling herself she really did need a few more pictures. Besides, the sun had just broken through, and while she was no weather expert, it surely would hold off a little longer.

"There's an inlet farther down with a nice clearing to set up a pretend camp," he added. "And it usually has decent phone reception."

Phone reception was all the convincing she needed.

"You're the expert," she said. And realized she meant it. For someone who'd practically raised herself—if one didn't count the revolving door of au pairs and boarding school staff—it was a foreign feeling for Charlotte to willingly give over control of her environment to another person. Yet, so far, she'd felt reasonably safe in Alex Russell's capable hands. Well, not in his hands, literally, but more than a few times, she'd looked at his strong, tanned fingers maneuvering the oar and wondered how many women on whitewater rafting vacations had volunteered to ride next to him.

"Just let me make sure I haven't forgotten anything." She pulled her laminated list of supplies out of the small pack strapped around her waist and ran her finger down each item.

"I thought we went over that thing several times already, back when we loaded the raft." They had, and he'd been extremely patient the first time she'd reviewed it. Now, though, she was getting the feeling he didn't appreciate her ability to always be prepared. Probably because he was rolling his head back the way Audrey did whenever Charlotte told the five-year-old to pick up her My Little Ponies before she could have dessert.

"We did, but I don't like to leave anything to chance."

"Well, it's not like we could simply row ourselves to the nearest department store in the event you forgot something. Besides, you haven't taken anything out yet, so it should all still be there, right?" He rubbed his hand against the back of his neck, the gesture similar to his grandfather's earlier, and Charlotte fought the impulse to reach up and straighten his collar.

"Hopefully." She smiled, but didn't apologize for her organizational skills. It only took a moment before she nodded and walked quickly toward the raft, getting her expensive new boots soaking wet in the process, since the filled raft was too heavy to pull entirely onto shore and had stayed shin-deep in the water. She had one leg over the side, but her sore arms and bulky life vest made it somewhat difficult to heave herself back in. She froze the second she felt his hands on her hips and suddenly her mistake in footwear wasn't the only thing she felt foolish about.

"Here you go," he said, lifting her up as if she was as light as one of her daughter's plastic toy ponies. Because she wasn't expecting the help—or her body's response to his touch—her knee jerked, causing her leg to slip on the outer edge of the bow. Without dropping her, Alex shifted his hands so they were cupping her rear end and gave her a final boost inside.

When she finally scrambled onto her seat, Charlotte didn't know what was warmer, the intimate places he'd touched her or her blushing cheeks. After Mitchell's betrayal, she'd vowed to never fall so easily for a man again. But there was something about the fresh air and the natural isolation of the land around them that must be drawing her to the reserved river guide. The self-discovery book she'd read about camping suggested that peoples' hormones were heightened and more animalistic when they were out in nature. Or maybe it was his rugged attractiveness combined with his quiet confidence that filled Charlotte's mind with the kind of lustful thoughts she shouldn't be having.

He secured the fishing line to the inside of the raft and Charlotte tamped down the shudder that threatened to erupt every time she caught sight of the lifeless, glassy fish eyes of his catch. Even though she was familiar with prepping all kinds of food, she normally didn't have to sit right next to something that had been alive just a few minutes before. To take her mind off the dead trout, the man's use of the word *dicey*, and the way his hands had perfectly formed around her curves, she decided she'd ask some background questions for her article as he took the inflated bench behind her and they paddled toward the middle of the river.

"Have you had a lot of women, Mr. Russell?" Charlotte's oar paused midstroke and she sucked in her breath, wishing she could pull the words back in with it. "I mean, are you used to women being with you?"

Oh, no. That hadn't sounded any better. Thankfully, she wasn't facing him and he couldn't see the embarrassment heating up her face.

"In what sense?" Captain Hot Hands back there

probably had plenty of urban females flocking to the wilderness looking for a little more adventure than what was offered in the brochure.

"You know what? That came out wrong. I was trying to ask about your clientele. I'm definitely better at answering interview questions than asking them."

"But you're a reporter, right?"

"Not really. I'm more of a lifestyle expert."

"What the hell is a lifestyle expert?"

"I'm not exactly sure, to be honest with you. I started out posting some recipes in my sorority's alumni newsletter—"

"Sorority?"

"Yes," she said, trying not to sound too defensive. Charlotte wasn't oblivious to people's skepticism and mocking tones when it came to things like Greek life or beauty pageants. But she also wouldn't apologize for her past or for the connections she'd made in that world, a world that had welcomed a very lonely girl when everyone else had shut her out.

"So," she continued, "I started getting follow-up questions and comments asking about ingredients, which turned into questions about household tips, which morphed into interior decorating. Pretty soon, I had my own blog about home entertainment and *Fine Tastes* contacted me about writing for them. But most of what I do is really just creating recipes and coming up with ideas for room décor and throwing parties. That sort of thing."

"So you're more about presentation than about substance?"

She jerked back her head and frowned at him. "That's probably the judgmental way of looking at it."

"Sorry," he said, his smirk back. "Nobody's ever called me judgmental before."

Charlotte didn't know if she necessarily believed that. She'd seen the skepticism in his eyes—before he'd quickly covered them up with his sunglasses—when they'd been talking about her sixth grade canoeing skills back at the put-in location. She'd also noticed the way he'd frowned at the brand new water-resistant performance pants she'd bought especially for this trip before suggesting that they reschedule. Sure, the man had been very patient with her so far today when instructing her how to paddle and how to angle her body when they'd hit their first set of rapids. But he also reeked of no-nonsense skill and leadership.

Well, technically, he reeked of aloe-scented sunscreen and cool water and something much more manly and musky and way too arousing. She purposely looked at the dead trout as a way to refocus her attention.

"Has anyone ever called you evasive?" she couldn't help the frustrated tone. "It takes forever to get an answer out of you."

"I'm sorry. Can you repeat the original question?" She didn't have to turn toward him to hear the grin underlying his words. He was teasing her about her awkward query and she sort of deserved it.

"Do you get many female customers?" Okay, so that wasn't what she'd really wanted to know, but it was the only way she could save face and not sound like she'd been speculating on his relationship status.

"Of course. In fact, we had our first bachelorette party last August. My dad led that group and said it was one of the wilder and more entertaining trips he'd ever been on. This time of year, though, it's mostly the adrenaline junkies and the experienced water enthusiasts who want to be out on the river. Later in the summer, when the current slows, we get a lot of families—usually on the lower rapids."

She seized on the word *families* because Charlotte would feel a lot less anxious about the narrow canyon ahead if she could imagine a raft full of boys and girls playing and frolicking in this same river. "So it's safe for children?"

"Absolutely, as long as they understand the risks and their parents keep an eye on them. I heard you mention child care earlier. I'm assuming you have kids?"

"Yes. Elsa is six and Audrey is five. They're currently with my friend Kylie Gregson back in Sugar Falls. Your grandfather said he knew her and would stop by and let them know that we'd be back tonight."

She felt the slight movement of him shifting in his seat behind her. "Pull your oar in for a second," he commanded, his tone not as playful as it had been a few moments earlier. "I'm going to try to move to the center of the channel."

She struggled with the conflicting desire to follow directions but to also be of assistance. "Shouldn't I help paddle us in that direction?"

"Nah, the current is strong enough that I just need to steer us that way. But if you don't mind, the line is slipping out of our friend there, and he needs to be re-secured before we hit the rapids and your glamping meal bounces out."

"Sorry, Trouty," she said as she tightened the clear string through the dead fish's gills, causing its mouth to gulp open wider. But just then the raft dipped and

Charlotte barely looked up in time to see a fallen tree trunk caught between two boulders.

"High side," Alex shouted and Charlotte froze. What did that command mean? "Jump to the other side," he yelled again.

But she must've been too slow because when she lifted up to move, a wave caused by the changing current slammed into them and knocked the boat sideways. Charlotte felt her left hip bounce on the rim before she toppled backward into the water.

Icy cold pins stung her skin, but the shock of the frigid river was nothing compared to the rolls of turbulent waves pounding into her and spinning her body around until she lost all orientation and all sense of control. Air. She needed air. Logically, she knew bubbles rose to the surface, but there were so many damn bubbles going every which direction. She clawed at the current, trying to find her way until she grew dizzy with exertion.

Her thrashing foot hit a rock with enough force to catapult her back up, and she barely had time to feel the cool air against her wet face when her life jacket was practically yanked over her head.

It took her several seconds to realize that Alex had just pulled her back into the raft and she was face to face with Trouty, whose eyes were probably less bulgy than hers were by this point.

"You okay?" Alex asked.

No, she wanted to shout, but her trembling lips wouldn't form the word. She'd almost drowned, almost orphaned her daughters. The unbearable thoughts of what could have happened churned inside her head, robbing her of speech. She'd never experienced such an all-consuming panic, such an intense fear. Yet all Charlotte could do was cough in response.

"Just hold still down there while I ferry us through this gate." Charlotte had no idea what he'd just said except for the *hold still* part. And if she could convince her rapidly heaving chest to do that, she'd be fine. Or so she told herself.

Alex had seen plenty of people tossed into the water and he'd seen plenty of people slow to recover from the shock. But he'd never seen anyone so shaken up after the experience. Of course, being the guide, he couldn't afford to stop the craft in the middle of a potentially dangerous situation to calm the passenger down. He usually let the others in the boat soothe the poor soul. But it was just him and Charlotte out here and Alex wasn't so heartless as to ignore someone still in emotional distress.

"Tell me how you know Kylie," he said, knowing the best way to get her mind off the incident was to keep her talking about anything but what was scaring her. It was also the best way to get his mind off the way the thin, wet fabric of her pants clung to her long shapely legs.

"We competed in the Miss Northwest pageant together," she replied, her voice sounding as dazed as her wide-eyed stare.

Heaven help him. A sorority girl *and* a pageant queen. Unfortunately, he'd been right and Charlotte Folsom was the exact type of woman he went out of his way to avoid. His already wet hands went clammy. So, maybe he hadn't been completely honest earlier when he claimed nobody had ever called him judgmental. Some of his best friends had married women just like the one trying not to hyperventilate on the floor of his raft, and those guys often laughed at his semijests that they'd crossed over to the dark side. The pretty women he'd dated in college required too much maintenance. The city women he'd refused to date required a fast-paced lifestyle he wouldn't wish on his worst enemy—or Commodore's worst enemy, since Alex usually got along with everyone. Charlotte was a combination of both—beautiful and urban—and probably used to the finer things in life. Actually, there was no probably about it. She was a lifestyle expert for a magazine called *Fine Tastes*. Enough said.

Not that there was anything wrong with those types. They just weren't for him. Just like the feel of Charlotte's firm hips and curvy rear end wasn't for him. Or for his hands. He'd felt her pause when he'd first touched her, wanting only to assist her into the boat after he'd secured the fish. Yet he'd experienced a tremor through his own body that had nothing to do with the frigid water. Had she felt it, too? Was that why she'd paused?

"How long was I under?" she asked, interrupting his inappropriate thoughts.

"Maybe twenty seconds," he said, then cleared his throat.

"That's all? It felt like forever." He'd fallen out of a few boats himself and understood the sensation. It was always an adrenaline dump when a person found out they were never in as much danger as they'd originally thought.

She propped herself up on her elbows. "How'd you catch up to me?"

"You didn't really get very far. The undertow helped. So, your girls are with the Gregsons?"

"Yes, do you know them? The Gregsons, not my girls. Obviously, you wouldn't know my girls since you've never met them. Oh, my gosh, my poor girls." When the woman's voice shook, Alex cursed himself for trying to talk about a pleasant subject. "What if I'd died and never saw them again?"

"Listen, Charlotte. Your children are fine. And you're fine. Focusing on all the 'what ifs' is no more productive than bouncing around in those rapids back there."

Charlotte lifted her head enough to peek over the side. "Are we past them, then?"

"Yes."

"Do we have to go through more areas like that one before we stop at that clearing you talked about?"

"Only two more."

She shivered, and he wasn't sure if it was just her subsiding panic or the wind that had picked up. Normally, they recommended wearing wetsuits this time of year because of the cool water temperatures. But because the more risky rapids were still miles away, he'd figured they could change into the uncomfortable things only if they decided to go that far down river.

He glanced down at her lips, which had gone from cotton candy pink to pale blue. Yet she didn't utter a single complaint. Alex was a firm believer that if some tourist wanted a firsthand experience of the land, they should be ready for all the elements Mother Nature could dish out. But Charlotte Folsom was also just doing her job, and even if he didn't appreciate the necessity of whatever a lifestyle expert was, he had to give the woman credit for her commitment and her work ethic.

He especially had to admire that her biggest concern had been for her children and he wondered if her daughters had any idea how lucky they were to have a mom who worried about abandoning them. Not everyone was as fortunate.

Besides, while he knew how to put up a good front and calm down a customer, Alex was pretty sure his heartbeat was still bouncing along at the same tempo as the rapids behind them. He talked a big game when it came to people being tough enough to survive the vast wilderness, but at the end of the day he alone was responsible for bringing this woman back to her daughters. It was a powerful responsibility and one he normally didn't take lightly—which made him feel all the more like a jerk for those initial judgments he'd made about her lifestyle and her wardrobe. It made him feel even worse for the thoughts he'd been having all day about wanting to put his hands on her.

But of the two guilt-inducing feelings, Alex knew it was in his best interest to remain skeptical and aloof. He'd never had to struggle with breaking his well-established rule about hooking up with the female clientele because he'd never been as attracted to one as much as he was to Charlotte.

He let out a ragged breath and felt his shoulders pull forward.

Maybe he should stop and let her change into some dry clothes, that is, if she'd packed an extra set of the name brand gear. And maybe he could take a second to get his own head back on straight and remind himself that she was just another customer. Just another woman.

"Listen, Charlotte, we still have about another hour or so to get to that spot I was telling you about. But, there's a place up ahead where we can pull out and you can dry off and regroup."

Alex knew better than to suggest that a lady might need some time to calm down. Growing up without a mother, he'd been a slow learner when it came to figuring the female species out, but by the time he got to college, he'd learned to avoid the high maintenance ones. And in Alex's opinion, most of them *were* high maintenance. Unfortunately, he couldn't exactly avoid the woman shivering in front of him.

"I really don't want you to have to go to any extra trouble for me. Especially because I never would have fallen into the water if I'd been paying better attention. But…" She hesitated long enough that he could hear her teeth chattering. "Would it be too much of an inconvenience?"

A few clouds had cleared, but Alex had lived on this mountain all his life and knew the weather could change on a dime. "Well, I'd prefer to pull out on the left bank, because the majority of access roads are on that side of the river."

"Is there anywhere to stop on that side?" She was sitting up straight, now, and even had an oar cradled in front of her. He followed her gaze to the craggy, sheer side of the canyon.

"Not for a couple more miles." Her nod was swallowed by another shiver. He had to admire her perseverance. Many inexperienced urbanites would've been complaining already. "Actually, this spot coming up on the right side wouldn't be a bad place to stop for a few minutes."

He saw the relief in her shoulders as she climbed back onto her perch and stuck her oar back in the water. It only took a couple of minutes to steer them onto a wide stretch of riverbank. Alex tied the raft to the branch of a fallen log, then held out his hand to assist a very wet Charlotte, careful not to allow himself to get too close to her again. Her fingers were rigid with cold and he doubted a quick change of clothes would do much to help elevate her body temperature. Yet, despite her quivering lips, she stood on the pebbled shore and stared at the lush green foliage in front of her.

"This is gorgeous," she said, then blinked a few times as if she couldn't believe what she was seeing. "It's so remote and untamed. I've never seen anything like it before."

Alex smiled, somewhat awed by her appreciation for the land, and his chest expanded as though he was responsible for its design. Since he handled the store and the recreational sports side of the business, his dad was usually the one to witness the tourists' first impressions of being completely surrounded by nature. In fact, Alex hated to admit it, but having been raised on the mountain, he was so accustomed to the great outdoors that he sometimes had to remind himself not to take it for granted.

"It *is* pretty incredible, huh?" Alex squeezed her hand, telling himself he was just trying to stimulate more blood flow through her freezing fingers. But when she returned the squeeze, he suddenly had to worry about his own blood flow. And the way it was racing to the part of his body just south of his waistband. He quickly dropped her hand.

Again with the inappropriate thoughts. She was a paying client and he'd never had trouble separating business from pleasure before. Sure, she was a knockout, but she was also from a world very different than his own. If history had taught him nothing else, it was to keep his distance from women like her.

"Too bad we can't do the photo shoot with this as the background." Charlotte's chattering teeth didn't stop her from smiling. But it *did* stop him from using his better judgment.

"You know what, why don't we take the pictures here?" For the hundredth time, Alex looked up at the sky and hoped the weather would hold just a little longer, because his good sense was slowly floating away. "I was actually thinking you could benefit from a little fire and if you can do your cooking thing while I set up a pretend campsite, we can snap a few photos and be back in the raft in an hour."

"That would be so incredible, if you're sure you don't mind." Her eyes were currently a deep shade of blue and he wondered how to make the violet hue return.

"Nah. To be honest with you, I'd be relieved to just get it all over with quicker and have Commodore meet us at that clearing I was telling you about." He pulled out his cell phone and looked at the screen. "Too bad we still don't have reception, otherwise, I could have him waiting for us when we got there."

"Since we're being honest…" Charlotte stretched her arms over her head "…I would rather wait on land than paddle through any more rapids."

It was a normal response for a person who'd never experienced the physical exertion and danger of paddling on one of the most unpredictable rivers in Idaho. Alex respected her candor, even if the admission didn't surprise him. It was also a good reminder that Charlotte Folsom was from the city and his body had no business reacting to her with anything other than concern.

"Here," he said, unhooking her waterproof duffel bag and handing it to her. "It shouldn't be too difficult to find a tree to hide behind and change."

A blush shot up her cheeks, bringing some much needed color to her cool skin. "How do you know someone won't see me?"

"This is national forest land and the surrounding thousand or so acres are prohibited to hikers and campers."

"So, we shouldn't be here?"

"I know the local rangers. If we get caught, they won't slap us with too big of a fine." He was trying to make a joke, but her eyes were completely serious.

"But we'd be breaking a rule."

"You've never broken a rule before?"

She bit her lower lip, her brows scrunched together as though she were trying to recall the answer. "Not knowingly. Besides, I think it would set a bad example for my daughters if they saw me doing something against the law."

"If it puts your mind at ease, Russell's Sports has a special permit allowing us access to the river and the areas near the shoreline. Unless we get too deep in the woods over there," he pointed toward the towering redwoods about a hundred yards away, "we're not breaking any laws. So, the sooner we get those pictures taken, the sooner I can get you back to your daughters and you can tell them about your great rule-following adventure."

Charlotte had looked skeptical until he'd mentioned her kids and then the woman couldn't move quickly enough up the bank and toward to the pine trees surrounding the tall grass meadow.

Alex admired her eagerness to be reunited with her children, refusing to think about other mothers who couldn't wait to ditch their kids and return to their lives in New York. Not that he was bitter about something that had happened over thirty years ago or anything.

He unloaded several of the dry boxes and carried them to the grass above. Then he returned to the bank to collect a few small boulders to circle around a campfire. He grabbed a small hatchet from the box of supplies and set out in the opposite direction of Charlotte. By the time he returned to the makeshift pit, he had enough dry branches and wood chips to get a small fire going.

Charlotte walked toward him, looking drier and much more relaxed than she had a few moments ago. She also looked more beautiful than she had when she'd stepped out of Commodore's Jeep. Her damp hair was darker and wrapped up into some sort of loose bun on top of her head, a fringe of bangs covering her forehead. The elastic headband was still in place, but her hair looked more natural, less formal.

From his kneeling position, he tried not to stare at the way the athletic fabric of her yellow, long-sleeved T-shirt clung to her small, pert breasts. Especially since he was pretty certain that her bra was drying with the rest of her wet clothes hanging off a nearby branch.

He struck the first match and got his thumbnail instead. Damn it.

Focus, Alexander. He heard his father's voice reminding him that the customers come and go, but the river and the land were always there and deserved his full attention and respect. He knew better than to let a woman distract him, especially while lighting a fire. Besides, it was better than Commodore's voice, which was a gruff, *Pay attention, son,* accompanied by a light smack across the back of his head.

"Is there anything you need me to set up before I start cleaning Trouty?" Charlotte asked.

He finally got a small flame going and blew on it a few times before responding. "You named our lunch?"

She leaned over his shoulder and looked at his wristwatch. It was well after three o'clock. "Technically, I named our dinner if we don't hurry."

Technically, if she moved any closer to him, he'd fall into the fire he'd just lit. He stood up a bit too quickly and the top of his head bumped into her chin.

"Ow," she said, at the same time he blurted out an apology.

"Are you hurt?" He took either side of her face between his palms and, after nudging her hand out of the way, studied her jaw.

He didn't know if it was the heat from the fire or something else that caused her face to warm up. But from the way she was avoiding eye contact with him, he had to wonder if she was reacting to his nearness the same way he'd just reacted to her tight shirt. Then he had to wonder why he cared.

"No, it's my fault," she said suddenly, taking a step back. "I'm usually not so accident prone."

"Good thing we have a well-stocked first aid kit, then." Alex wasn't good with lighthearted banter. Or with women who expected too much from him. He needed to get back to what he did best. "So, tell me where you want me to set up the tent."

"I was thinking by those trees," she said, pointing to the smaller ponderosas away from the river. "It's too bad the sun isn't setting, otherwise we'd get an awesome shot of the light coming through the branches."

"Trust me, we don't want to be here after the sun sets."

Her eyes grew into perfect circles and now looked more violet than blue. "Why? Are there bears and wild animals?"

"Probably. But I was actually referring to being on the river at night with a storm coming. And right now, we're burning daylight."

"Right," she said, and set to work going through the container holding cooking supplies. But he noticed the way she stole glances toward the forest, as though she was worried an unwelcome visitor would join them for their meal.

Alex began pitching the tent, then decided the pictures would look more realistic if he set up some sleeping bags and a lantern inside. He'd had his doubts about Charlotte's ability to cook something over an open fire rather than in a fancy state-of-the-art kitchen and those concerns doubled when he realized she was stopping every few minutes to take pictures of what she was doing with her smart phone. But when the mouthwatering scent of pan-fried fish reached his nostrils, he began to rethink his initial concerns.

Or maybe he was just hungry. He knew he should've

had the stuffed French toast at the Cowgirl Up Café in town this morning instead of the simple bowl of oatmeal. Good thing his dad always taught him to pack extra dried food supplies, even for these day trips. He didn't care how indigenous Charlotte Folsom wanted her staged meal to appear. If it didn't taste good, he wasn't eating it.

Alex made his way toward the fire to investigate whether he'd need to resort to freeze-dried tuna, but before he got there, a booming roar sounded and a flash lit up the gray sky. He saw Charlotte jump at the crashing noise, right before he saw a bolt of lightning hit one of the lower hanging trees by the river bank.

The tree splintered in two, with the heavier side falling in slow motion—right toward where he'd moored the raft.

Chapter Three

Don't panic. Don't panic. Don't panic.

Charlotte wasn't sure if it was Alex talking to her or her own psyche. But it was good to remember that she wasn't all by herself.

The raft was gone. The rope snapped when the tree landed on it and sent the inflatable boat rushing down the river. She wasn't one to be a pessimist, but if that wasn't bad enough, the overhead clouds finally gave way and opened with a sheet of rain. "What do we do?"

"Grab the food," Alex said over a loud clap of thunder. "I'll close the dry boxes and meet you in the tent."

"Wait, what if lightning strikes the tent?"

"The poles are fiberglass, not metal. And it's better than sitting out here in the wide open. Besides, it usually goes for the tallest thing in an area and since the tent is by a grouping of smaller trees, we shouldn't be in too much danger."

"Did you see what happened to the last tree it hit?"

"Charlotte, take Trouty and get in the damn tent, please."

Rules and lists and directions made her feel safe. Having someone with her who knew the rules and how to give directions made her feel even safer. She pulled the sleeve of her shirt over her hand and picked up the skillet, which was still warm. As she ran toward the open tent, she felt a sense of peace come over her. Again she thought about the book she'd read right before embarking on this trip. In *Our Natural Souls*, the author spoke of how, hundreds of years ago, people with a lot less resources survived a lot worse conditions than these.

She took one steady breath and then another. This situation was only temporary and they'd get through it. In fact, Charlotte bet people from all over the world would pay Russell's Sports big money for exactly this type of adventure, being forced to commune with nature. The rain wouldn't hurt her, it would only add depth to her article. She needed to focus on the positive.

By the time Alex ducked into the tent, he almost looked surprised to see her sitting cross-legged in the center. She was calmer than even she would've thought possible. And if she hadn't been, then she'd at least had years of etiquette classes to teach her how to pretend she wasn't on the cusp of a panic attack.

"I suppose there's some sort of plan set in place for these types of unexpected events?" she asked.

"The plan is that we hole up from the storm and wait for someone to come get us."

"How do you know they'll find us?" Whoops, that anxiety was creeping back into her voice.

"Why wouldn't they?"

She wanted to hear answers, not more questions.

She held herself perfectly still, looking at the flapping material of the tent and hoping this thing could withstand what felt like hurricane strength winds and rain lashing against it. "What if they don't even know we're gone?"

"Com knows when to expect us at the pickup location. Even he will miss us after a while," he said, fiddling with the lantern he'd brought in with him. "As long as it doesn't interfere with the *Deadliest Catch* marathon he planned to watch this evening. Besides, someone will spot an empty raft eventually, and hopefully notify the Forestry Department."

The light flared to life and it wasn't until then that Charlotte realized how dark it had gotten outside. "So they should show up any time?"

"Well…" Alex wasn't looking at her and the pit in her stomach sank deeper than she had into the Sugar River.

"Tell me." She might be nervous, but it wasn't like she was some emotional basket case who couldn't handle the truth. She'd certainly weathered worse figurative storms than this and knew it would be best to arm herself with all the facts.

"When we don't show up, or when someone finds our raft, they'll realize we got stuck out here and ground crews will start looking for us on the left side of the river because that's the easiest for them to access. Since we're on the right side, it might take a bit longer."

"But they should be able to see us from the water, right? This tent is bright orange."

"Nobody will be on the river with weather conditions like this. Even a rescue crew." She tried not to shudder at the word *rescue*. That made things sound so much more dire. "If the lightning does move on and the wind eventually calms, it's still too soon to tell how much rain has already dumped down, which means there's a risk of potential flash flood conditions. Then, when you add debris and falling trees and rocks to the mix, it makes the river way too dangerous. And that's just during daylight." He looked at his watch.

She felt the curves of her fingernails dig into her palms. "So, level with me, Alex. How long do you think we'll be out here?"

"Honestly, it just depends on the storm. But the good news is that we have plenty of supplies out there, hopefully not getting too wet. And we have shelter. Things could be a lot worse."

His attempt at a positive sentiment matched her own, but with more confidence. She flexed her fingers. They would be perfectly safe. Just like her daughters were perfectly safe back in Sugar Falls. And as long as she didn't think about how this was the first time she'd been away from her girls, perhaps she could think of this as a working vacation. What a great story she'd have to tell her children, and her blog followers, when she got back.

"Are you cold?" she asked, seeing that his flannel shirt was soaking wet. Focusing on someone else distracted her from worrying about whether she'd remembered to pack Audrey's multivitamins or Elsa's miniature neck pillow.

"I'll be fine once I get dried off a little bit." He began tugging at the buttons and Charlotte squeezed her eyes shut, knowing that once she saw him shirtless, she'd never be able to forget the image.

Maybe she *shouldn't* be focusing on him. She racked her brain for something to take her mind off the man undressing a few feet away from her, then remembered the pan of food sitting beside her. "I don't suppose you grabbed any dishes or silverware?"

"Nope," he said. She looked up at his bare torso, but her gaze didn't go any higher than his chest, the golden skin taut against the contours of his muscles. Yep. Looking at him had been a big mistake. Before she made things worse by lifting her gaze to his face, her eyes shot away and focused on the baseball cap he'd tossed to the corner. She hadn't seen him without the thing on and found herself desperately hoping that he was bald with some sort of misshapen skull that would detract from how stupidly attractive he was from the eyebrows down.

Charlotte peeked up to see a head full of thick, brown hair, damp and slicked back from his forehead. Hell. The guy was completely perfect. And she was trapped in tent with him and her own racing heartbeat.

Actually, she wasn't trapped at all. She could unzip this thing and walk out any time she liked. As long as she didn't mind getting electrocuted or pelted in the face with icy water. But a bit of fresh air would clear her head. "I'll just run out and grab some plates and utensils real quickly. Do you know which box they're in?"

"I don't think leaving shelter right now is a good idea," Alex said. "I know you probably take table set-tings and all that fancy dining stuff seriously, but maybe your readers would be interested in how good campfire meals taste when eaten straight from the pan."

"You mean with our fingers?"

"That's how people used to do it before they invented silverware."

"Right." The last thing she wanted was for him to think she was some sort of stuck-up princess. Actually, she shouldn't want him to think about her at all. "Here, you first."

"Wait, tell me what all you foraged," he said, one eyebrow raised as he looked at the skillet. "Not that I don't trust you, but there are plenty of poisonous plants growing around here and…"

"Actually, I studied a book on local plants before I came out. I didn't use anything I wasn't completely sure about."

"Of course you didn't," he chuckled. "You're a rule follower and a list maker."

"And I'm an excellent packer," she said, trying to sound lighthearted while reminding herself that the girls would be perfectly fine without her for one night. But when he squatted down next to her, his brow wasn't the only thing raised. Her pulse had skyrocketed and she was in danger of becoming lightheaded.

"What does that mean?" he asked.

"It means that I brought some dried seasonings with me in case we couldn't find any."

"It really is all about the staging and presentation, isn't it?"

"Your tone is implying that I'm some sort of big faker."

"Aren't you?"

This guy must have some serious trust issues. Not

that she didn't. But she didn't go around voicing them to strangers. She doubted he was trying to insult her directly, but she was getting the feeling he didn't think too highly of her. "Not if I'm honest about the added ingredients," she said, wishing she didn't care about whether he liked her or not. But wanting to fit in and belong was an old habit that resurfaced in stressful moments like these. "I did find ginger, which I was expecting, as well as shortstyle onions and camas. I brought along the dried mustard, though, and the rosemary and parsley for the vegetables."

He studied the small roundish-shaped bulbs she'd browned in the pan along with the fish. Charlotte had never eaten camas before, but her research said it had a potato-like flavor. He popped one into his mouth and chewed for a few seconds before swallowing. "I have to say, I'm pretty impressed."

Her heart fluttered against her rib cage at the compliment. This was why she cooked. Because even if people didn't appreciate her, they always appreciated her food.

She looked at the way the light sprinkling of hair covered his chest before tapering down into a narrow line over his stomach and almost admitted that she was pretty impressed herself.

She squeezed her eyes shut and prayed for strength because being surrounded by all this nature was sure bringing out her most uninhibited instincts. Not only had she never eaten straight out of a pan, she'd also never shared a meal with a half-dressed man.

He sat beside her and she put the skillet between them, thankful they both were facing the zippered door and not each other. Their temporary shelter had been advertised as a three-man tent, but there was barely enough room for her overactive imagination in this small space, let alone another person.

He ate a bite. "Wow. This is good."

"Thank you."

"I mean *really* good."

"Did you think it wouldn't be?"

"I didn't want to doubt you, but Com says to never trust a skinny chef."

"I'm not sure if that's supposed to be a compliment."

He let his grayish-green eyes travel over her again and she felt her nipples tighten in response. "It's definitely a compliment."

"Which part?" she asked. "The not trusting me part or the too-skinny part?"

"I didn't say *too* skinny. In fact, I'd say you were just right."

Suddenly, this tent felt like a portable steam sauna. Tiny curls sprang to life around her hairline and she adjusted her elastic headband—which wasn't as sturdy as her normal tortoiseshell one, but went better with this casual outfit—to keep the wayward things from tickling her face.

They needed to get back to a neutral topic.

"Speaking of your grandfather, Commodore gave me a little history of the waterfall and some of the local legends." There, that was a safe enough subject.

"Are you sure you mean Com?"

"Yes. That *was* your grandfather who drove me up here to meet you, right?"

"Yeah, but the old guy barely says more than two sentences at a time if he doesn't know you. And if he *does* know you, you'll wish he *only* said two sentences."

"Really? He talked quite a bit, actually, about how he and your grandmother moved to Idaho after he got out of the Army because they wanted to start a family away from the…what does he call the suburbs?"

"The land of maggots on a grizzly bear?" he suggested.

"Yes, something like that. Anyway, he said his bride fell in love with the falls the moment she set her eyes on it and told him she'd rather have a boat than a house."

"Now that definitely surprises me. Not his description of the suburbs, of course. I won't tell you what he calls it when he's not in mixed company. But Com never brings up Granola. Of course, he never lets anyone talk him into smearing lip balm on himself, either, so maybe he doesn't mind you too much."

"Doesn't mind me *too much*? Is that supposed to be another compliment?"

"It is." He took another bite of fish and rolled one of the camas in her direction.

"Who's Granola?" Charlotte asked.

"That's what I used to call my grandma. She passed away when I was seven and it's just been me, Com and my dad ever since."

His eyes turned the same shade as the moss-covered rocks she'd slipped on near the riverbank earlier when she'd been cleaning Trouty. And if she wasn't careful, she could find herself slipping straight into their hidden depths, as well.

All her life, she'd looked for human connections, for someone to open up and show themselves to her. That's what happened when one's parents ditched their only child to be raised by hired caregivers. But Charlotte had learned with her ex-husband that emotions could be faked. Tenderness could be imitated. And women searching for love and acceptance could easily be fooled. It was the reason she cherished her relationship with her daughters so much. They were the only real things in her life, the only people who needed her and wanted her as much as she needed and wanted them.

Charlotte took a bite of the potato-like vegetable, hoping the less she said, the more he'd tell her about himself. The guy hadn't been much of a talker, initially, and if there was anything that reminded Charlotte of her lonely childhood, it was long silences. She needed to get him to say *something*. After all, they had nothing but time out here until someone found them. Yet Alex didn't seem to want to be the focus of the conversation.

"What about you?" he asked. "Where did you grow up?"

"Mostly in San Francisco. I attended boarding school in Connecticut and then back to Stanford for college. Have you lived in Sugar Falls all your life?"

"Yep. I went to the University of Idaho in Moscow, but I usually came home on the weekends."

"Have you ever wanted to leave? To travel or live somewhere else?"

"Nope."

It was going to be a long evening and an awkward night if the man refused to add much to the discussion.

"I recently read this book called *Our Natural Souls…*" Charlotte paused briefly when she saw Alex roll his eyes to the roof of the tent. What was that dramatic response all about? "Anyway, the author talked about how important it is for everyone to go on a journey to find themselves."

"Hmm," was his only reply. An awkward silence grew between them and she wondered how they would ever get through the night if the man refused to talk. He ate in silence while she pulled her journal out of her small pack and began writing some notes on her preparation of the fish, making adjustments for the cooking time based on how close the pan had sat over the campfire.

An hour must have gone by before Charlotte had run out of things to write to about. It grew darker outside and he switched on a battery-powered lantern, fiddling with the settings. When she couldn't stand the silence any longer, she looked over at him and saw a fleck of dried rosemary stuck to his bottom lip.

"Here." She reached out her hand to wipe it off. But when her finger touched his mouth, a spark sizzled to life inside her and she drew her arm back quickly. Based on the way his head whipped around, she wondered if he'd felt it, too. "Sorry. You had something… uh…right there."

He rubbed the back of his hand over his mouth. "Thanks."

"So what do people normally do this time of evening out in the middle of nowhere?" she asked.

"That would depend on if we weren't locked together inside a tent." The way his deep voice said the words made her think of all the things they could do *inside* said tent. And the way their bodies could become locked together.

She shook her head. "What about outside?"

"The best part of camping is being outside," Alex

said, his eyes flickering to life. "There's the campfire, which is where all the best stories are told. There's just something so basic and natural about sitting in front of a roaring fire, it makes people want to open up and let their guard down. Plus, food tastes better when it's prepared and eaten out in the open, the way our ancestors had to make it."

His voice was an invitation to relax and listen to the passion he felt for the land he clearly loved. "Then there are the games. When I was a kid, we'd play capture the flag, send codes with flashlight signals, go on nighttime scavenger hunts—which forces you to rely on your other senses since it's too dark to see. And don't even get me started on the stars. When I'm back at my house in Sugar Falls, I can go a week without looking up and giving the constellations a second thought. But out here, you're surrounded by the night sky. Being blanketed by all the twinkling lights is better than any old comforter back home, and you fall asleep thinking about all the adventure and beauty that awaits you the next day."

"No wonder people come out here to find themselves," Charlotte said.

"You know all that finding yourself nonsense is only for people who are lost." He took a sip of water out of the Nalgene bottle he'd brought into the tent earlier. Then he offered her a drink. She didn't realize how thirsty she was, but sharing the container somehow felt more intimate than everything else they'd shared so far.

She tried not to think of where his lips had touched and instead thought back to her years at boarding school, and before that to her childhood with parents who were never around. "Maybe all of us are a little lost."

"I'm not." His voice was firm, his eyes focused intently on the seam above the tent's entrance. "I've always known that I belong in Sugar Falls and I don't need a burned-out political speech writer making money off her book about some vacation-turned-spiritual-journey she took thirty years ago telling me what I already know."

He seemed pretty familiar with the book, which confused Charlotte, because most people raved about *Our Natural Souls*. "But the author is so brilliant and what she says about finding one's inner home is completely moving. It really changed my life."

"The author was a complete phony and a BS artist."

The anger in his voice made Charlotte gasp. "How do you know?"

"Because she was my mother."

"The rain's let up," Alex said, rising to his feet before Charlotte could wrap her pretty little head around the admission he'd never spoken out loud to anyone else. "I think I'm going to check on the dry boxes and see which supplies we can fit in the tent for later tonight."

The wet flannel of his shirt was no colder on his skin than the chill he'd gotten when she'd first brought up the book that was never mentioned in his house. Still, he shrugged on the clammy fabric and walked out into the drizzle before he said something else too revealing.

Surviving the elements wasn't a problem for him. Unfortunately, surviving the close quarters with a beautiful lady who wanted to talk about journeys and changes in perspective and all that emotional crap made him pray for a rescue chopper to drop down from the dark, moonless sky overhead. But no sane pilot would risk that, even if there was a lull in the storm, which there currently was.

He knew he should've listened to his gut and not his grandfather's damn knee when it came to the weather. If he had, then he wouldn't be stranded out here all alone with that woman. A woman who made him think about things he'd cut loose long ago. Alex stomped over to the nearest dry box and hefted it up on his shoulder, carrying it closer to the tent.

Why did Charlotte have to bring up that stupid book? Sure, the thing might've been on the *New York Times* bestseller list for most of 1990 with an Oscar-award-winning movie released the same year Alex started middle school. But what none of Mariah Judge's devoted fans and followers knew was that the physical and emotional journey the woman so touchingly chronicled never once mentioned the son she'd conceived with her much younger river-rafting guide. Or how that child never fit into the world she'd been so quick to run back to.

Hell. Alex hated thinking about his mother and he rarely allowed himself to. But something about Charlotte Folsom brought to mind every single maternal notion he'd never allowed himself to crave.

At least, not since Granola had passed away. That was another thing. Why'd Charlotte have to bring up his grandmother, as well? Or be such a damn good cook? That food she made was acting like a truth serum and he hadn't been able to stop himself from divulging his entire life story to a total stranger.

But at least talking to her had kept him from looking at the way her shirt hugged her breasts. Or how her long legs stretched out in front of the sleeping bag as they'd shared that pan of food. It also kept him from thinking about how those same legs would feel wrapped around his waist.

He stumbled over a pinecone he hadn't seen in the dark and then kicked the offending thing as far as he could, imagining it was a soccer ball full of his attraction for the pretty mom—who'd probably gone back to writing notes in her journal back inside the tent. Not giving Alex or the feelings she'd stirred up inside him a second thought.

He found the second dry box right where he'd left it, near the now-drowned campfire, and carried that one over, as well, wishing for some other physical task to take his mind off things. He opened the box and grabbed the first aid kit and a few bottles of water.

Being in a tent, living off the land, was second nature for Alex. So he wasn't worried about food or supplies or even the weather. He was mostly concerned with how he'd be able to spend the entire night next to Charlotte Folsom, who was not only sweet and nurturing, but had those soft lips that made him think of trying out her fancy potted lip balm. And the most expedient way for her to apply it. He'd trade his own Chapstick for a chance to feel her mouth on his.

Inappropriate, Russell. She wasn't some bored tourist looking for a good time with the first river-rafting guide who came along. Charlotte Folsom was here because of her job, because she was a dedicated employee.

In fact, she was a mother—a single mom, possibly—who couldn't wait to get back to her kids. And she was completely vulnerable and out of her element.

He grunted when he dropped the heavy dry box next to the small tent that seemed to shrink more and more each time Alex thought about returning to it.

"Can I help?" Charlotte asked, peeking her head out of the zippered door. He wanted to let out a curse, but it wasn't the woman's fault that he couldn't keep his hormones in check. Although, it *was* her fault that the way she'd meticulously organized every single thing in these heavy boxes was making him feel out of *his* element. He could imagine her pulling her little laminated checklist out of that fanny pack thing she'd kept strapped to her waist and wanting to go over their supplies. For the thousandth time.

"Here," he said passing the first aid kit to her. His knuckles brushed against her soft fingers and he suddenly forgot how cold it was out here in the damp wind. "I figured we should pull some of the essentials out and keep them inside with us for the night."

She set the kit down near one of the sleeping bags and then reached out to take the bottled water. Alex was more careful about making contact with her hands again, but he was running out of excuses to avoid the tent. He grabbed an extra battery pack for the lantern and slipped it into his pocket.

"I'm going to take a short walk over to those trees," he said, holding on to one of the bottles of water and a small Ziploc bag containing his toothbrush.

"Why?" Her always curious eyes were wide and he wished it wasn't dark so he could see what color they were now.

"To use the men's room."

"What men's… Oh." Now he wished he could see the blush rise up on her cheeks. "Maybe I should go with you. I mean, not *with* you, but to the ladies' room version."

He heard some rustling around and then the flapping sound of the tent door as she unzipped it fully and climbed out. She held a small pink neoprene toiletry pouch and seemed to be checking the contents before tucking it under her arm and grabbing another bottle of water. He imagined she was the type of person who carried around dental floss, hand sanitizer and wet wipes with her wherever she went.

As they walked into the copse of trees, she kept close to him, so close that she bumped into him when she jumped at the sound of a red squirrel scampering across the ponderosa branch above them. It was another good reminder that he and Charlotte were worlds apart. And with the way his pulse skyrocketed every time she was near him, he needed all the reminding he could get.

He stopped and grabbed three football-sized rocks, then carefully stacked them on top of each other. "I'll meet you back here in a couple of minutes."

"Okay." He handed her a small flashlight and they went their separate ways. When he returned to the designated cairn, she was already there waiting and holding something out to him.

"Here," she said as he reached his hand out reflexively, only to feel a squirt of cold gel plop into his palm.

He nodded toward the travel-sized bottle of disinfectant. "You really are a city girl, huh?"

"Yes. But I'm also a mom. I usually have half the medicine cabinet packed into my purse."

And there was another reminder that this woman wasn't only from a different world, she was also someone's mother. She couldn't be any more off-limits to him if she were a nun.

She wrapped her arms around her torso and took a big, shuddering breath. He put a hand on her shoulder. "Are you okay?"

"I think so," she nodded. Then stated with more force, "I will be. I need to stop worrying about whether or not the girls have everything they need and keep in mind that Kylie is a mom as well and my children are in good hands."

"They really are." Alex used his finger to raise her chin up so she could see the reassurance in his eyes. "Your daughters are probably having the time of their life at their lake house."

"But what if nobody finds us?" The concern on her face was better than the blind panic he'd seen right after pulling her out of the water. But he was overwhelmed with the need to put her fears to rest.

"Charlotte, you need to trust me. I'll get you back to your girls, okay?"

"Okay," she said and this time he felt her nod. His finger had moved from her chin and was cupping her cheek and it was only a matter of time before Charlotte realized that he was standing way too close to her. He forced his feet to take a step back and dropped his arms.

"Your kids and husband must be lucky to have you taking care of them." Man, that sounded like the cheesiest attempt to fish for information. But Alex really needed to hear that she was married, or had a boy-friend, or anything to cement his belief that she was off-limits.

"Thanks. The girls are still young enough to ap-preciate it, but I have a feeling that by the time they hit those tween years, they'll accuse me of smother-ing them."

"And your husband? Does he appreciate it?" Crap. He hadn't actually asked that had he?

"Ex-husband. And I haven't spoken to him in over two years so I really don't know what he appreciates." Her voice grew quiet, losing the animated tone she nor-mally used whenever the subject of her daughters came up. Which must mean that she didn't want to talk about the guy. As interesting as that was, he should probably take Commodore's advice and mind his own business.

"Do you think the storm's passed?" she asked.

As though to answer for him, the sky opened up with a heavier batch of rain. "Nope."

By the time they got back in the tent, Alex's shirt was soaked through. Granted, it had been wet to start with, but there was no way he could keep the thing on all night and not freeze to death. Same thing with his cargo pants.

"What are you doing?" she asked, causing him to pause with one sleeve off.

"I'm taking off my clothes."

"Why?"

She sure used that word a lot. "Because they're wet. And I'd suggest you do the same."

"But I don't have any more dry clothes."

"You don't need clothes to sleep. In fact, your sleeping bag will keep you warmer if there isn't a layer of material to detract from your body heat."

The soft glow from the lantern made the blush on her cheeks more pronounced. Thank goodness for this week-old stubble covering his jaw and his own flush of embarrassment, because his blood was hot enough to burn through his skin.

"Here," he said, reaching for the light hanging from a carabiner overhead. "I'll turn this off first and we can face away from each other."

"Okay." Her voice was whisper soft and he'd never heard a more alluring sound in his life. Maybe it wasn't awkwardness heating his body from the inside out, but plain old fashion lust. He kept his back to her as he peeled his damp pants off and laid them out flat on the tent floor.

He'd been wrong a few seconds ago.

The sound of her removing her clothes was way more alluring than her voice. He disregarded his earlier advice about sleeping completely in the buff and kept his boxer briefs on, climbing into his sleeping bag quickly so she wouldn't see the evidence of his arousal. Thankfully, it was too dark to see anything. Although that realization didn't do anything to diminish his desire to catch a glimpse of her.

Waiting for the sound of her zipping up her sleeping bag took forever. When it finally came, he let out a breath and commanded his body to relax. Neither one said a word, and he wondered if she was as completely aware of him as he was of her.

After a few minutes, he heard something other than the booming roar of thunder outside.

"Are you cold?" he asked her.

"No."

"Then why are you shivering?"

"I don't know."

"Are you afraid of the thunder?"

"Not exactly." But he could hear the tension in her voice.

"Of bears or wolves?"

"I wasn't until you just reminded me of them."

"Then what are you afraid of?"

She paused for so long, he wondered if she'd fallen asleep. "It's embarrassing."

"Listen, Charlotte. It's just you and me and a few bears out here. What happens on the whitewater rafting adventure trips, stays—"

"I hate being alone," she interrupted.

"But you're not alone. I'm with you."

"I know, and I'm glad for that. What I mean is that it's just so vast and solitary out here in the wilderness and I don't like being away from the people I love. Sorry, you must think I'm crazy."

He just thought she was too used to the crowded city—which *was* somewhat crazy. "Don't feel bad about it. Not everyone is made for the outdoorsy life."

"Alex, is Mariah Judge really your mom?"

Where in the hell had that come from? "Do we have to talk about this? I thought we were talking about you and your hang-ups?"

"I'd rather talk about yours. It helps me not to think of mine."

He sighed. "Yes, she gave birth to me, but she was never my mom. That's the ironic part of her book, not that I would ever lower myself to actually reading it. She came on a spiritual quest to find herself, but doesn't mention the baby detour on her life journey or the fact that she discovered that motherhood wasn't for her. She painted herself to be all about self-awareness and open to change, but after her trip was over, she couldn't wait to get back to her hotshot life in the city. Really, she sold a lie to millions of people."

"And I bought it," Charlotte's voice sounded resigned. "You'd think that after my ex-husband and his blatant dishonesty, I'd become better at not just hearing what I want to hear and seeing what I want to see."

Whoa. That was a loaded admission and one Alex wanted to learn more about. But the rain had somehow reactivated the rich, floral fragrance of her hair and a throbbing of awareness—low and deep and intense—was warning him not to let things get any more personal.

'We sure are a dysfunctional pair, aren't we?" he said. "I'm sure we can come up with something more pleasant to talk about."

Actually, he preferred not to talk at all. The sooner he fell asleep, the sooner he could stop imagining what those full, cotton candy lips of hers would taste like.

"You know," she said, her voice lighter as if something finally occurred to her. Maybe just having someone to talk with had calmed Charlotte's fears. "It's scary out here, but if I don't let myself get swallowed by my worry over my daughters, it's also a little liberating, isn't it?"

"I guess so." Personally, he thought there was no better experience on Earth than to be all alone, communing with nature. "And remember what I said about making sure you get back to your girls. You're not alone."

"Alex, would you mind if I put my sleeping bag closer to yours?"

Only if he wanted to be up all night inhaling the fragrance of her shampoo and imagining her naked skin nestled into her down-filled nylon cocoon. "I don't know if that would be such a good idea."

"I promise I'm not trying to make a move on you."

"Why would I think that?" he asked, too defensively. The answer would've been obvious if she could see how tense his body was at that exact second.

"Oh, come on. I'm sure you have women on these trips throwing themselves at you all the time."

"Actually, my dad usually runs these trips."

"That's what Commodore said."

"I try to stay away from the women looking for too much adventure," he continued.

"That's what Commodore said, as well."

He leaned up on his elbow. "Really?"

"No. But I'm sure he would've if I'd asked him." She lifted her head and rested it on her palm as she looked at him.

Hmm. After seeing the way the gruff old mountain man let her coddle him with lip balm and lectures about wearing a hat in the sun, Alex didn't doubt his grandfather would've told the inquisitive woman anything she wanted to know.

"I'm sorry about bringing up your mom," she said, growing more serious. "I had no idea."

"It's fine."

"But it makes sense why you wouldn't want to get involved with the customers."

"That doesn't have anything to do with it. I just like to keep my distance from women in general." He sure wasn't proving the truth of that statement because, as he said the words, he noticed that he'd somehow managed to scoot his sleeping bag closer to hers. "I like my life the way it is."

"Of course you do," she said, in that sexy, soft whisper.

Another clap of thunder shuddered through the trees outside, and he found himself grasping the edge of her bed roll, tugging it toward him. He heard her indrawn breath, the same one she'd made when he'd placed his hands on her hips to lift her into the raft earlier today. But, just like then, she didn't pull away.

"You live in your world and I live in mine," he said, talking more to himself, wanting reassurance that, despite their physical proximity, he still had some emotional boundaries left.

Their faces were inches apart. She slowly brought up her fingers and he sensed her hesitation as she tentatively reached out to touch his jaw. Yet, this time, her caress felt anything but maternal. "You said it yourself, though, right? What happens out here stays out here?"

But what exactly was happening? He could navigate the wild mountain terrain in the snow without a GPS, but he'd never trusted himself to read women very well unless they provided him with a clear course.

"Are you sure about this?" he asked, not wanting to question what exactly *this* was.

"Just tell me the rules." Her thumb traced the outline of his upper lip.

Of course she wanted rules. "No," he said, kissing her finger lightly. "You tell me."

"But I've never done this before."

"Neither have I," he admitted.

"Okay, rule number one," she said, those full lips of hers practically touching his. "When they find us, we go back to our worlds. No strings attached."

"No strings attached," he agreed, before pressing his mouth to hers.

They never got to rule number two.

Chapter Four

It had been way too long since Charlotte had felt the weight of a man pressing against her body. It had been even longer than that since one had rained hot, tender kisses down her neck. One minute Alex Russell, sexy river guide extraordinaire, had been naked in his sleeping bag. The next, he was naked inside of hers.

The down-filled nylon embraced them like a cocoon and held their bodies together. When he'd told her that she would warm up quicker if she took her clothes off, she'd mostly listened. But going from the dorm rooms to the sorority house to the townhome she'd shared with Mitchell—who had always worn a shirt to bed—and then her daughters, meant she'd never slept in the nude before. So she had kept her damp cotton camisole and panties on, and now she wished she'd been a bit more impulsive.

Alex's cool, rough palms set off sensations against her rib cage as he slid her shirt up over her head. Her bun fell loose and she had to fight the urge to clap her hands to the top of her scalp to smooth down the wild curls. She felt more exposed without her trademark headband in place than she did shirtless.

"I was fascinated by your hair the second I saw it," Alex murmured. Charlotte had spent thirty minutes blow-drying and straightening it this morning—as she did every morning—and could only imagine how much different it looked now after being dunked in the river. "I knew all that tamed smoothness was hiding some-thing better underneath."

Maybe it was just the soft romantic glow of the lan-tern, but his eyes drank her in. The muscles in her neck melted, causing her head to fall back and her chin to lift up toward him. Like her hair, Charlotte suddenly felt untamed and wild.

Alex toyed with another strand before dipping back down to kiss her. And, oh, what a kisser he was! His mouth was as adventurous as his personality, navigat-ing her lips, exploring her tongue and trailing his way down to her chest. He was in no hurry, probably be-cause they had the whole night out here, but Charlotte had never experienced such a rush of pleasure and was eager to make the most of this one-night adventure.

She shifted her legs to make more room for him, causing his hips to settle firmly between her thighs. She moaned when the rigid length of him nestled against the thin fabric of her panties, and she tried to wrap her legs around his waist before realizing the sleeping bag was prohibiting her movements.

"Hold on," he said, his voice sounding as ragged

as her heartbeat felt. Alex yanked so hard on the zipper, the sound of the nylon material ripping echoed in the tent.

Cool air breezed over her bare skin as he rolled off her and reached for something in the corner. She squinted at the white box with the red cross. "Are you hurt?" she asked, quickly sitting up and springing into caretaker mode.

"No. I just need to get something out of the first aid kit."

"Like a bandage?"

"No. Like this." He held up a small square package and it took several seconds for Charlotte to figure out what the thing was. When she did, heat stole up her face and she prayed he hadn't noticed her puzzled expression. Of course she knew what a condom was, but she'd never actually seen one up close. When they were dating, Mitchell had refused to use one and Charlotte had always taken birth control pills—or, at least, she had until those antibiotics from a bout of strep throat had rendered them ineffective and she'd gotten pregnant with Elsa.

She lay back against the silky fabric of the torn sleeping bag and squeezed her eyes shut, forcing all thoughts of her daughters and her ex outside of the tent. She was about to have sex with a stranger—spontaneous, rugged, outdoor sex with an incredibly good-looking stranger. None of her research had prepared her for this experience, but for once in her life, Charlotte Folsom wasn't going to overplan or overthink things.

Alex tore open the package, and though Charlotte was tempted to watch in complete fascination, she took advantage of his distraction to ungracefully shimmy out of her underwear. All those poise lessons for all those beauty pageants were wasted here and the only thing she could do was hope that she didn't appear foolish. Why wasn't she better at this sort of thing? Should she lie there flat or should she attempt a seductive pose? It turned out that she didn't have time to do either.

He returned to his position over her, but he didn't kiss her again. Instead, he studied her face as if he needed confirmation that she was okay with what they were about to do. She bit her lip, sucked in a shaky breath, then simply said, "Please."

Alex's arms were trembling as he held himself over Charlotte, trying to take things slow. But the second she said "please," he couldn't hold himself back any longer.

She arched her hips and he slid into her as she moaned. He almost shuddered with his own release right then and there, and pulled out a little, just so that he could get himself under control. But the resistance of Charlotte's calves locked around his waist propelled him back inside. Another moan—from her or from him, he wasn't sure—and then they were moving together, building a rhythm until he gave one final plunge and felt her contract around him before calling out in ecstasy.

When his throbbing pulse finally slowed its jackhammer speed, he gazed down at her. Her eyes were closed and a small smile played upon her lips. He might not be boyfriend material, but he wasn't opposed to satisfying a woman in other ways. Of course, he hadn't expected how passionate or responsive she would be, and Alex was surprised at his own body's inability to hold back—and his sudden urge to keep her close.

She made a little gasping sigh when he rolled off her and gathered her against his side. She nestled against him and for a quick second, he experienced a moment of panic that Charlotte Folsom was the post-coital snuggling type and might expect more from him than one night of lovemaking. Then he thought about how different their lives were and how smart Charlotte seemed to be. Nah. There was no way she was reading too much into this, and he shouldn't be, either. This was definitely a one-time thing for her—for them both—and he might as well lie back and enjoy the comfort of sleeping in the great outdoors with a beautiful woman.

His skin was damp with sweat and the cool air wasn't doing either of them any favors. He tried to pull the top of the sleeping bag over them, then gave up when it wouldn't reach.

"Here," she said, moving away from him and toward his empty bed. His initial instinct was to pull her back, to suggest that they sleep together. Then he realized how needy it would've sounded. In the end, he didn't have to say anything, because she unzipped the other sleeping bag and spread it out over both of them. He rolled onto his side, wrapping his arm around her waist.

"When I asked you what kinds of things people did at night while camping," she said, scooting her rear end against him, "you never mentioned this."

Laughter burst out of Alex's chest, the first time in a long time he could remember honestly feeling it so deeply. When she joined in, the throaty sound—or maybe the curve of her round bottom pressed so close to him—caused another shot of desire to ricochet throughout his body.

He lifted her curly hair and kissed the nape of her neck, and then neither of them were laughing.

Despite making love for most of the night, Alex lazily woke up to the sound of chirping birds and the promise of a stunning sunrise. Charlotte was still asleep, or at least pretending to be, so he left the tent first thing to make use of the bushes and then start a fire. The smell of the camp smoke mingled with the cool, crisp mountain air and Alex took a deep breath, feeling more at home in this natural environment than he ever would in some fancy house.

Not that anyone was offering him a fancy house.

The unmistakable sound of shuffling and movement from inside the tent let him know that Charlotte was awake and reminded Alex that it would be a long day if she was feeling uncomfortable about what they'd done last night. He didn't do well with tension or awkward silences, which was why he didn't do serious relationships. Though he was always up-front with the women he casually dated and sometimes went to bed with, he'd never really stuck around once the sun came up.

But when she emerged with her sleepy eyes and tousled hair, Alex couldn't resist pulling her in for another kiss. He caught a glimpse of her smile before she pressed her hand over her mouth and mumbled that she needed to brush her teeth. So at least they'd gotten the initial embarrassing morning-after pleasantries out of the way.

They both tended to their respective grooming needs, then met back at the campfire, where Alex gave her an even more thorough kiss and she responded with as much heat and passion as she had last night. There was nothing uncomfortable about the way she fit in his arms and then there was the fact that making out was way easier than talking. But as much as he wanted to spend the morning wrapped up with the beautiful and sensual woman, there was plenty of work around camp that needed to be done. When he finally pulled himself away he asked, "Can I make you some coffee?"

"Why don't I make *you* some?" she responded, matching spots of pink coloring her cheeks. "I'm not used to having anyone else cook in my kitchen."

Alex looked around at the small fire pit and the plastic tote bin of cooking supplies. "*Your* kitchen? My, aren't you territorial."

She shrugged her shoulders and smiled unapologetically. "Mine. Mother Nature's. Doesn't matter. It gives me a sense of purpose and it's one of the few things I'm good at out here."

"Actually, there's something else you're pretty good at," he said, then nodded toward the opening of the tent.

He expected another blush, but instead she replied, "That's nothing compared to my coffee," then grinned.

Alex doubted anything could be better than what they'd done in that tent, but he was too busy enjoying this confident side of her. He sat back on the log and watched her dig through the bin of supplies and pull out a stainless steel percolator. Her movements were precise and decisive as she used bottled water and the fancy coffee grounds she must've packed for the trip. The only drawback to watching her work was seeing her use her smartphone to take pictures, since it reminded him that this wasn't supposed to be some relaxing sex-filled vacation. It also reminded him that he'd crossed a line last night—a couple of times—when he would've preferred to go on forgetting that he was supposed to be acting in a professional capacity right about now. But there would be time enough for recriminations later. As long as he didn't let things go any further.

Man, he needed a healthy dose of caffeine if he was going to manage an ounce of common sense around this woman.

The aroma coming from the percolator was enough to bring him to his knees and he watched as she deftly poured coffee into two tin mugs, then staged them on a tree stump next to a few loose pinecones. Charlotte bent down and snapped some more pictures. Just when Alex thought he was going to have to wrestle the phone away from her, she stood and handed him a cup before joining him on the log.

"Still no service," she said, wiggling the electronic device before setting it down between them. But she didn't look as worried as she had yesterday. In fact, she looked well rested and well loved. Her face was tilted up toward the clear sky, which was still tinted with shades of orange and pink and her smile was as pure as the sunrise. "It's even more beautiful out here today than it was yesterday."

He picked up her phone.

"What are you doing?" she asked. She held her coffee in both hands, blowing on it before taking a sip.

"Taking a picture of you."

She shifted her cup and ran some fingers through her hair. "Why?"

"Because I just realized that you were the one behind the camera yesterday, which means there aren't any photos of you. Your readers might enjoy seeing exactly how gorgeous you are first thing in the morning."

"Trust me," she said, pointing to the messy curls piled on her head. "Nobody wants to see this."

"*I* want to see it," he said simply, then tapped on the shutter button.

She rolled her eyes. "I bet Martha Stewart never gets stranded on a river with her hair all a mess and no make-up."

"Well, if she did, I bet her coffee wouldn't be half as good as yours." It was true. The taste was bold with layers of rich flavor and a smooth finish. He would've said as much but he didn't want to sound like a pretentious snob.

"I'll tell her you said so. If I'm ever lucky enough to be in the same room as her." She leaned over and pressed her lips on his quickly. "You do wonders for my ego, you know."

Warming up, Alex smiled. "I also bet Martha Stewart's kisses aren't half as good as yours, either." Then he pulled her in for another make-out session.

Charlotte wrapped her arms around his neck and with the fresh shot of caffeine traveling through his bloodstream and the thumping of his heartbeat, Alex realized they might go for round four out here in the wide open. Wait. That wasn't his heartbeat. That was…

He broke away just as a helicopter rose above the copse of trees behind them.

Charlotte jumped up, knocking her cup over and frantically waved her hands above her head. "We're down here," she shouted several times, and Alex was too choked up with annoyance over the timing of the

Forestry Department's arrival to point out that the chopper pilot couldn't hear her.

He dug his booted foot into the still-damp ground as if he were one of the kids on his little league team who'd been tagged out at second base. He wasn't ready to be rescued yet. They'd only had one night together, and once they returned to civilization, all of this would be over.

"Why are they just hovering over us like that?" she yelled. "Don't they see us?"

"The clearing is too small for them to land. They're probably holding their position so that the rest of the rescue team knows where we are."

Just then, a Polaris RZR broke through the bushes. The all-terrain vehicle was splattered with layers of mud and Alex guessed the Forestry Department had spent quite some time yesterday evening looking for them. Commodore was strapped into the passenger seat and, with his perpetual frown and his arms crossed over his stocky body, looked almost disappointed that they'd found them so early in the day. His grandfather loved the thrill of a good search and rescue mission and it hadn't been a full twenty-four hours yet.

Alex recognized the driver as one of the fish and game wardens and waved as they drove up. The relief on Charlotte's face was obvious, and as soon as the men asked them what had happened, she turned into a chatterbox, talking a mile a minute. Which was good, because Alex wasn't ready to quit pouting just yet. A couple of forest rangers in another off-road vehicle pulled up, along with Scooter and Jonesy, two old cowboys and volunteer firefighters, riding in on horseback.

What was once their serene and romantic clearing

in the woods was now the center of a damn party. The obnoxiously loud helicopter finally flew off and Alex started taking down their tent, the routine work distracting him from answering questions and thinking about how excited Charlotte was now that all these people were here—how eager she was to get away from him. A walkie-talkie crackled to life and a ranger spoke into the thing before passing it to her. At the sound of her friend's voice on the end, the strong woman he'd just spent the night with burst into tears.

Suddenly, his gut dropped with guilt. What kind of selfish jerk would mope around like he had, wishing they could've stayed out here another day? Of course she was worried about her children and her magazine article and her perfect life back home. And he couldn't blame her.

Alex just wished he could've held on to her a little longer.

Chapter Five

The all-terrain vehicle was like a golf cart on steroids and their ride through the forest of towering pines was rocky and unsettling, each jarring bump playing havoc with Charlotte's nerves. She was harnessed into the backseat beside Alex, and when they hit a small boulder, she grabbed his leg and clung to him. He stroked her hand and she relaxed her fingers enough for him to lift her palm up and place it in his own.

Her emotions—along with the ATV—bounced all over the place. Seeing that helicopter had flooded Charlotte with relief. Then, when the off-road rescue vehicle showed up, she'd been brought to tears. Logically, she'd known all along that she had been perfectly safe with Alex and that eventually someone would find them. But Charlotte hadn't been fully convinced that all was well until she'd heard Kylie's voice crackling through the walkie-talkie. That was when she'd known the ordeal was over and that she'd get to see her children again soon.

A couple of older gentlemen on horseback offered to stay behind and clean up their temporary shelter, and Charlotte and Alex were whisked away—back toward civilization. Yet, holding hands with her stiff and stoic river guide in the back of this off-road machine, she also realized that their return meant their short-lived love affair was over. A small part of her heart deflated in disappointment because she'd likely never see him again after this.

For the past twenty or so minutes, the only sound she'd heard was the revving engine of their souped-up rescue vehicle. Then, as they approached the ranger station, the wailing of a siren caught her attention and she spotted several white news vans. Alex's firm grip around her fingers was slightly reassuring, but he still didn't say anything. And, really, what was there to say?

"What's with all the cameras and reporters?" she shouted, trying not to flash back to the worse day of her life. Five years ago, she'd come home from the park one day, pregnant and with a one-year-old in tow, to a similar scene surrounding her stately family home. But that time, her husband was being led away in handcuffs.

The driver yelled over his shoulder. "Press found out a couple of people went missing last night and they've been camped out here to report on the rescue mission."

"But we were gone less than twenty-four hours," Alex finally spoke up. "That's not exactly newsworthy."

Commodore huffed. "It is when the editor of *Fine Tastes* magazine starts calling all his news cronies."

Oh, geez. Charlotte should've known Neal would've

jumped on the opportunity to sensationalize this story. She scanned the crowd for her boss and anyone else from her magazine crew. However, her eyes didn't get far after landing on a tall redheaded woman heading their way, two little girls running in front of her.

"Mommy!" Elsa cried the second the driver stopped. The six-year-old launched herself onto Charlotte's lap.

"Peep! Peep!" Audrey shrieked. Her younger daughter held one arm akimbo and the other curved upward.

"She thinks she's a teapot," Elsa said, and rolled her eyes. "She won't come up here unless you lift her by her handle."

Charlotte gave her older child another tight squeeze before unstrapping herself and climbing out. She picked up Audrey, who was prone to imagining herself as inanimate objects and then going into such deep character, she refused to talk. "A teapot, huh?"

"Peep," the little girl said before collapsing into a fit of giggles as her mother tickled her. She pulled Elsa in for a three-way hug, not bothering to wipe away the tears streaming down her face. Charlotte had tried not to let her own imagination get away from her, but in the past twenty-four hours, there had been several times when she worried that she'd never see her sweet children again. She kissed their round cheeks and stroked their matching brown hair, drinking in the scent of their watermelon-scented shampoo.

An ambulance was backed up and a pair of medics rolled a gurney over to them. "Did you get hurt, Mommy?" Elsa asked, her big hazel eyes wide with fascination. Her oldest was overly curious and Charlotte didn't want to give the child any reason to worry.

"Nope." Charlotte kissed her daughter's forehead. "Mr. Russell kept me perfectly safe and sound."

"I just bet he did," Kylie Gregson said, her tone a little too smug, her smile a little too knowing. The tilt of her friend's perfectly arched brow caused a thread of guilt to coil around Charlotte's stomach. Certainly it wasn't *that* obvious that she and Alex had done more than just sleep in a tent together.

"Who's Mr. Russell?" Elsa asked. "The guy with the little stick in his mouth?"

"That's Commodore Russell," Kylie explained. "The younger Mr. Russell is his hunky grandson. Come on. I'll introduce you to them while the paramedics take a look at your mom."

"Peep, peep, peep?" the little teapot called out.

"Audrey wants to know what *hunky* means," Elsa translated, loudly enough for Alex and the rest of the news cameras to hear, as she and her sister followed a laughing Kylie.

Charlotte, wishing she could sink into a hole to escape her embarrassment, allowed the female paramedic to assist her into the back of the ambulance. Although she felt perfectly fine—physically, at least—the enclosed vehicle would provide a small amount of privacy so she could make her emotions—if not her hair—presentable again. She answered the medic's questions and was surprised to find that her blood pressure was a bit elevated. Her pulse was also above normal—although whose wouldn't be in this situation?—and she was starting to get hungry, but otherwise, Charlotte was perfectly healthy.

"We're going to give you a ride to Shadowview,"

said the woman, whose name was Garcia, according to her ID badge. "It's the nearest hospital."

Charlotte shivered and tried not to think about her appendix surgery when she was eleven years old. Her daughters had been born at a state-of-the-art birthing center, and besides attending a ribbon-cutting ceremony for a new reconstructive surgery wing named after her mother at Bay Area General, she avoided hospitals at all costs. The thought that she might be admitted—and separated from her girls again—caused a knot of panic to wedge in her throat. "But I feel fine," Charlotte explained.

"And you look fine. But it's procedure to run some tests and have you screened by a doctor, just in case."

"Is Mr. Russell going, too?" Charlotte hoped her voice didn't sound needy.

"You mean Alex?" Garcia was an attractive woman, and since she was from the same small town, it would only be natural for her to be on a first-name basis with the guy. But that didn't stop Charlotte's scalp from prickling with a sense of jealousy. All she could manage was a nod.

"Yep. He'll have to get medically cleared, too. In fact, since you're both able to walk and sit on your own, we'll probably transport you together, if neither of you mind." Garcia looked past her. "And speak of the devil."

Charlotte whipped around so quickly, she knocked her elbow into the defibrillator case mounted beside her. Alex stood at the open back doors, the other paramedic next to him.

"You got room in here for one more?" he asked.

"As long as it's you and not your cranky old grandfather," Garcia said, then extended her hand to help pull him up into the rig. "Commodore still hasn't forgiven me for making him wear that oxygen mask after he competed in the log-rolling contest at the Lake Rush Lumberjack Games last year."

"I'm beginning to think the old guy's brain has been lacking oxygen for a while. I just listened to him shout at two reporters and threaten to run over one of the camera guys with the Forestry Department's Polaris." Alex gave Charlotte a tentative smile. "How you holding up?"

"I'm fine." The look in his eyes said he didn't necessarily believe her. Charlotte would have to work on her tough girl act, but she was too emotionally drained at this exact second to care. "I definitely don't need to go to the hospital."

"You sound like my grandpa." He took her hand in his again and squeezed it, the simple gesture more encouraging than any tests the emergency room doctors might administer. "Kylie wants to know if she should meet us there with the girls."

Blood drained from Charlotte's face and she shook her head "No. I don't want them to see me in a place like that. It'll scare them."

It was the same thing Mitchell had said about the jail where he'd been held during his trial. At first, she'd been relieved at his selfless explanation because she didn't want to have to sit in a prison visiting center with her toddler and newborn and pretend everything was normal. But after all the lies unfolded and the fog of his betrayal cleared, Charlotte realized he wasn't protecting anyone but himself. She'd gotten the divorce papers days later—with her ex-husband giving up all his parenting rights.

"Hmmm. Will it scare *them*? Or will it scare *you*?" Alex's question brought her back to the present.

Both. It would frighten Charlotte, and that would terrify her daughters. Instead, she snapped back, "I think I know my own daughters, Alex."

Her voice sounded defensive—even to her. But she was entitled to show a little stress after what they'd been through, including their very public rescue. Charlotte hadn't anticipated the helicopter and the bumpy ATV ride, but she really hadn't expected all of the news cameras. Maybe she was being so snippy because she was in shock. Perhaps seeing a doctor wasn't such a bad idea, even though the memory of being admitted into one of those colorless, sterile hospital rooms all alone made her feel like she was a helpless nine-year-old all over again.

She took a deep breath and tried not to look at Alex's wounded expression. "I mean, the girls are a bit on the sensitive side and it will upset them to see me hooked up to all those machines."

"Charlotte?" Alex stared at her until she met his eyes. "One of your sensitive daughters just asked me if it was easier to kill a grizzly bear with a bow and arrow or with a gun. The other is riding around on my grandfather's shoulders and pretending to pour scalding hot tea on the different reporters."

She pressed her lips together and looked out the open doors. Raising little ladies wasn't for the faint of heart. And neither was being a rational adult. "Okay, so I hate the thought of spending time in a hospital and I don't have the energy to put on a brave face in front of them."

"Fair enough." He squeezed her hand, much the same way as he'd squeezed her shoulder last night in the woods. Why was he always doing that? It wasn't like she needed him to protect her or to reassure her. She was used to taking care of herself. But after she kissed the girls goodbye and told them to behave for Kylie, Charlotte's fingers found their way between Alex's, and during the entire forty-five minute ride in the back of the ambulance, they remained interlocked like that.

Commodore had followed them down the mountain and, not being one to willingly enter a hospital, either, left one of the store's Jeeps in the parking lot before catching a ride home with a buddy from the VFW. It only took a couple of hours for both Alex and Charlotte to get a clean bill of health and be discharged. Alex shuddered to think how much longer their stay would've been if he hadn't pulled Charlotte out of the cold river current when he had.

Or how much longer the bones in his hand could've withstood the pressure of her fingers every time a nurse came in to check on them. The panic on her face when he'd saved her yesterday was nothing compared to the expression of terror when the lab tech took a routine blood sample. Her aversion to hospitals rivaled even his grandfather's, and Alex had to concede that it was probably a good thing her daughters hadn't witnessed her stress.

"Are you hungry?" he asked as they walked toward the Jeep. He'd bought a package of Pop-Tarts from a vending machine in the ER waiting room, then watched as the Gourmet Queen sniffed at a piece before taking a tiny bite. She'd devoured the rest and he'd had to buy more.

"Starving," she admitted. "That pastry thing you gave me was good, but it must've been full of sugar because it barely took the edge off."

Of course it was full of sugar. Had she never had junk food before? He opened the car door for her. "There aren't a lot of restaurants near here, but there's a great café in Sugar Falls if you want to grab a late breakfast."

She didn't answer right away—probably trying to think of an excuse to cut bait and ditch him. The ringing of her cell phone saved them both from dealing with the inevitable rejection. She pulled it out of her tote bag—thank goodness Kylie had brought a change of clothes and her purse to the ranger station—and looked at the screen.

"It's my editor," she explained. "I have to take this. Hi, Neal."

Alex climbed behind the steering wheel and started the engine. As he drove out of the parking lot, he tried not to listen to the one-sided conversation with Neal—the dumbass who'd alerted the media and was responsible for all those news cameras.

His chest filled with a cold dread at the thought of what the bad publicity would do for his family's business. Losing a raft and getting a client stranded in a thunderstorm was bad enough. But having it plastered all over the six o'clock news definitely wasn't going to have the customers blowing up the reservation line to schedule potentially risky rafting tours.

"I was able to get a few pictures," Charlotte said into the phone. It wasn't like Alex was trying to eavesdrop on what she was saying to her editor, but they were in a car. It wasn't like he could just pull over on the highway and hop outside to give her a little privacy. Not if he wanted to get back to Sugar Falls anytime soon.

"I'll try to work on it tomorrow, but I don't know how soon I'll be able to get it to you. Uh-huh… No. I'll double check. There was only one meal. I doubt the readers will buy that, Neal… No… No. Not going to happen."

There was more talking coming from the other end of the line and Alex was tempted to grab the phone and tell the pushy guy to back off for a few hours and let the woman recover. But Charlotte had a job to do and Alex had a business to save. They both needed to get back to reality.

Rule number one was that they'd go back to their worlds. They'd both agreed to no strings attached. Normally, in his life filled with extreme sports, ropes and cables were a good thing. So then why did he now feel like he was scaling a rock wall with no harness?

"Okay, Neal. I'll try. I was planning to be home on Sunday. Of course I'll be back in time for the Black and White Gala. That's still three weeks away… No. Don't come out here… I promise, Neal. Have I ever not had something completely under control? Fine." Charlotte disconnected the call, then let out a frustrated sigh.

Alex's muscles were tense with curiosity, dying to ask what her editor wanted. But he needed to let it go before he found himself running to her rescue again. Charlotte was a smart and strong woman. She didn't need him to fight her battles. And he didn't need her to…well, he didn't need her for anything.

"Should I drive you back to Kylie's?" he asked, hoping she'd forget about his offer to take her to the Cowgirl Up Café. Better to just say goodbye now before either of them started thinking of what could never be.

"That's probably for the best." Charlotte smoothed her hair before resecuring it behind another one of those ridiculous headbands she'd found in the expensive-looking purse Kylie had brought her. "Neal wanted me to get started on the article right away so they can post a teaser on the website tonight."

"Did you tell Neal to shove it?"

"I tried to. And then I remembered that burying myself in work is the best way for me to get back to normal. Right after I spend a few hours cuddling with my girls."

Alex turned off Snowflake Boulevard, which ran through the center of downtown Sugar Falls, and entered Kylie's neighborhood. He was good friends with her husband, Drew, and spent Thursday nights playing poker at their house with several other men in town. But he doubted they'd be meeting up tonight.

Charlotte fidgeted with her seat belt. "I never really got the chance to thank you for taking me out on the river and for saving my article. For saving my life, even."

He was pretty sure she'd already thanked him for that. With more than just words. But he wasn't about to bring up sex when she was clearly champing at the bit to put the whole experience behind her. He hadn't even pulled into the driveway and she'd already gathered the handles of her oversized leather bag as if she was going to jump from the Jeep before he could put the thing in Park.

"So, you'll be flying out soon?" he asked, knowing he was stalling for time.

"Originally, I'd plan to stay through the weekend, write my article and then maybe take a few days off to spend time with Kylie."

He'd shut off the engine and turned toward her, but she wasn't quite meeting his eyes. He thought about offering to see her while she was in town, but his brain was screaming at him that a clean break was for the best. It was bad enough that he'd slept with a customer, he shouldn't try to date her, as well.

The urge to say something pressed against the back of his throat and was fortunately overridden by the urge to pretend as though he wasn't going to spend the next twenty-four hours thinking about her.

He exited the car and walked to the passenger side; however, she'd already let herself out.

"You don't have to walk me to the door." Her smile wasn't necessarily cold, but it was polite and her tone was final.

"So this is goodbye," he said.

"I guess," she replied, and put out her palm as though she intended a formal handshake.

He reached past her outstretched fingers, grabbed her waist and kissed her instead. Her purse fell to the ground as she wrapped her arms around his neck and opened her lips to his. Alex put all his feelings into that kiss, every single thing he wanted to say. *When you're back in your big city world, I hope you'll think of me. I've never met anyone like you and I'll never forget the time we spent together. I know it's crazy, but I'm going to miss you.* And with the way her tongue was passionately thrusting against his, she was responding with everything she needed to say, as well.

He finished with two more soft kisses, then pulled back and said, "Take care."

She touched her swollen pink lips, then readjusted her headband. She picked up her bag and gave him a small wave before walking toward the house. He stood by the car, commanding his still-tingling legs not to follow her. Was this how his dad had felt when his mom walked out of their lives?

Of course not. His dad had probably been in love, while this was just a physical connection. Alex didn't even know Charlotte Folsom and he definitely shouldn't be standing there watching her walk away from him. It was prolonging things. Making him think about what could never be. She didn't turn back, and maybe it was better this way. No drama, no broken hearts, no strings. It was a clean break.

Alex pivoted on his foot and was almost to the Jeep when the front door was thrown open.

"Hey, Mommy!" The older daughter—the one who actually spoke with real words and had fired off questions at him a mile a minute—yelled from the front porch. "Aunt Kylie said she talked to Mr. Commodore and told him we'd cook dinner for them on Saturday night. She said it's all arranged. Did you know there are three of those guys and Aunt Kylie said the middle one is the hunkiest of all? Oh, hi, Mr. Russell. You're gonna love our dinner we make you. My mommy is the bestest cook."

He sucked in a breath before forcing a polite response out of his mouth. "I don't know how I could say no to an invitation like that." Seriously. He truly had no idea how to say no without sending everyone's suspicions into high alert on why he'd avoid a home cooked meal with the woman he'd just spent the night with.

Crap. So much for not prolonging things. In about forty-eight hours, he was either going to have to find an excuse to stay home or he was going to have to say goodbye all over again.

Chapter Six

"Sorry we have to do the thank-you dinner over here," Charlotte said to Commodore and Vic Russell two nights later. She was standing in the small kitchen of their mountain cabin with a cardboard box full of prepped food and wondering how she'd let her daughters and her best friend talk her into this.

"Are you kidding?" Alex's father asked, a gentle smile on his face. While Charlotte was partial to his son, Kylie and Elsa had a strong argument for Vic being the hunkiest Russell man. He resembled Hugh Jackman's older, better-looking brother, and it was easy to see why Alex's mother might have fallen for him. "I can't remember the last time we had a famous chef cook for us, let alone do it in our very own house."

"Charlotte's not a chef, Dad," Alex said, his face now clean-shaven and his full lips more evident, bringing heat to every place on her body those lips had touched. But even without the scruffy five-o'clock shadow, his rugged good looks were still readily apparent in his green flannel shirt and a pair of jeans that looked tailor-made for his long, lean legs. "She's a *lifestyle* expert."

The skin on the back of Charlotte's neck prickled at his patronizing tone and she wondered if he was put out to have her and her daughters at his family's cabin. Kylie had assured her that all three of the Russell men were looking forward to her making dinner for them and had convinced her that it would be the height of impropriety to not properly thank them for saving her life.

Yet now Charlotte wasn't feeling all that welcome. At least, by one of the three Russells. She hated the thought of being an unwanted guest, but for the life of her, she couldn't think why Alex would be made uncomfortable by her presence. Unless he thought she was shamelessly throwing herself at him. Charlotte blew her bangs out of her eyes and fixed her headband, praying that wasn't what he was thinking. After all, it wasn't as though she was the one who'd planted that kiss on *him* two days ago in the Gregsons' driveway and stirred up all those emotions she'd tried to leave behind at their impromptu campsite.

She'd attempted to say goodbye like a normal, civilized person who planned to never see their one-night stand again—which wasn't something they'd taught back in boarding school. Yet now she was here in his house with both their families, trying to act like she didn't know what was under his soft flannel shirt or how his warm skin felt against hers.

"As long as it's not your grandfather's cooking, I'll take it," Vic told Alex, then turned back to Charlotte. "So, how's Kylie feeling?"

"She's slightly better," Charlotte replied to the middle-aged and friendlier Russell, wanting to talk about anything but the man's son. "Unfortunately this afternoon, Drew and their twins came down with whatever bug she had, and since the girls didn't want to cheat you guys out of your promised meal, we decided to bring the dinner to you."

Actually, Charlotte had decided nothing of the sort—her well-meaning friend and eager daughters had done so on her behalf. But now that she was here, she was determined to play the role of good host. Or guest. Or whatever she was. Lord, she would feel more at ease if everyone would just get out of this tiny kitchen and let her do her thing.

"Hope you didn't bring the germs to us, too," Commodore said around the toothpick in his mouth, as he picked up a container holding the tiramisu truffle cupcakes Charlotte had baked this morning and sniffed them.

"Com, germs run in fear of *you*." Alex took the dessert box out of his grandfather's hand and stashed it on top of the refrigerator.

"Hey, Mommy." Elsa pulled on the fabric of Charlotte's blue sundress, a look of wonder in her six-year-old eyes. "Did you see all the pretend animals they have on their walls?"

"Those ain't pretend, dumpling," Commodore said. "They're just stuffed."

Charlotte took a deep breath, then bit her lip. Taxidermy wasn't something she was ready to explain to her young daughters just yet. Instead, she busied herself with redoing the lopsided buttons on the girl's pink cardigan.

Elsa seemed to ponder the older man's words before putting her hands on her hips. "Well, whenever it's time to clean up our rooms, Mommy says stuffed animals count as toys and we have to put them away. So maybe we can just hang ours up on the walls, like the Mr. Russells do here."

A pang of apprehension squeezed Charlotte's rib cage because it just dawned on her that where there were hunting trophies, there might be guns. "Honey, where's Audrey?"

Elsa let out a dramatic sigh. "She's pretending to be a teddy bear back in the stuffed animal room."

"I thought she was a teapot," Commodore said.

"Well, now she's a stupid bear," her older daughter replied.

"Watch your language, Elsa."

"Is *bear* a bad word?" Alex asked, his tone now playful as he winked at Charlotte over her daughter's head.

"No, but *stupid* is. We're not allowed to say stupid because stupid's a bad word. So don't say stupid, okay?" Elsa not-so-innocently batted her eyes every time she said the forbidden word. Alex's lips twitched. It was going to be a long night.

"Is there anything I can do to help you in here?" Vic asked.

"Uh, no. But thanks. Alex, may I speak with you for a second?" Charlotte didn't want to offend their hosts, but she also needed to make sure her daughters would be safe while at their house.

"Dad, Com, why don't you take Elsa and Audrey outside and show them my old tree fort?"

"I've always wanted one of those," Elsa said, then yelled to her sister in the other room. "C'mon, Audrey. They're gonna show us the giant doll house in the tree outside."

"It's a *fort*," Commodore corrected. "No dolls allowed."

"What about teddy bears?" Elsa asked, jerking a thumb toward her little sister. Audrey, arms spread wide, did a stiff-legged walk into the kitchen, looking more like a zombie than a plush toy.

"Fine," Commodore said, as Vic tossed Audrey up on his shoulders. "As long as they know how to shoot a bow and arrow."

Both girls whooped and Charlotte tried not to squeeze her eyes shut. A couple more hours. She needed to keep it together for just a little longer. "I don't think that sounds too safe. My children aren't used to…"

"We won't use real arrows," Vic interrupted. "Don't worry. We're experts at teaching kids about the outdoors."

Charlotte took another deep breath, then nodded because who wouldn't trust a sweeter, slightly older Hugh Jackman? "Okay, just be careful, ladies."

"And speaking of experts…" Commodore suspiciously eyed the other containers she'd already pulled out as Vic and Audrey headed toward the door. "Make sure you tell her about the fruits and vegetables, Alex."

Then the old man gave his grandson a pointed look before following a chattering Elsa out the back door. When the screen slammed behind them, Charlotte tried not to think about the fact that she was alone once again with Alex.

She couldn't very well talk about what happened the last time she'd cooked a meal for him. So, instead, she tried for a neutral topic. "I should've asked if your family had any allergies or food restrictions."

"For Com, it's not a restriction so much as an avoidance."

"To fruits and vegetables?"

"Only the kind not from a can. He doesn't trust anything without preservatives. So, did you want to talk about my grandfather's dietary quirks or was there something you needed to tell me?"

"Right." How could she have forgotten that she'd actually orchestrated getting him alone so that she could speak with him? "I don't know the most delicate way to put this because I know you all are more comfortable with dangerous outdoor activities, but I just wanted to make sure that all your guns and weapons and anything like that were locked up."

"Of course." Alex crossed his arms over his chest. "Just because we live out in the wilderness doesn't mean we're wild savages. Com has always taken safety very seriously and passed that down to us."

"I didn't mean to imply otherwise, but as a mother, I just needed to double-check."

"I get it. And I appreciate the fact that you're a concerned mom. But you don't know me all that well if you think I'd let a couple of children run around my house if it wasn't safe."

She didn't really know him at all. And now she needed to soothe his ego. "I'm sorry. You just didn't strike me as the kind of guy who hangs out with a bunch of kids."

"Then you'd be pretty wrong. I coach everything from Little League to youth basketball, and every summer my family runs an outdoor day camp for boys and girls."

Charlotte sucked in her cheeks. Wow. She hadn't seen that coming. Although, she probably should have. The guy had been incredibly patient with her out on the river, and his dad and grandfather had been great with her daughters so far. However, she'd grown up as an only child as well and assumed that, like her, he hadn't been exposed to too many kids. She really needed to stop making assumptions about Alex Russell.

Several moments of awkward silence ticked by as she tried to summon every hostessing skill she'd learned in those mandatory etiquette classes in boarding school. But he was the one who finally rescued their conversation. Just like he rescued everything else. "You didn't have to do all this."

"Do all what?"

He gestured toward the ingredients she'd set out on the faded red Formica countertop. "This thank-you dinner or whatever it is. You've already thanked me."

Heat stole up her cheeks thinking of exactly how she'd shown her gratitude that night in the tent.

"Not like that," he said, as if he'd sensed the direction of her thoughts, which was even more embarrassing. "I meant… Oh, never mind. What are you planning to cook, anyway?"

Her shoulders dropped, relieved to finally talk about a subject she was more familiar with. "I'm doing an antipasto platter with marinated and roasted vegetables, Mediterranean olives, capicola, and prosciutto. Then I've got an arugula and parmesan salad followed by herbed gorgonzola-stuffed cannelloni in a braised short rib ragu. I was going to do lemon garlic broccolini as a side dish, but since your grandfather isn't a fan of vegetables, maybe I'll just serve the rosemary focaccia, instead."

"Sounds pretty fancy." There went that patronizing tone again. She'd liked the guy so much better when it was just the two of them out in the wilderness and he was trying to reassure her that everything would be okay.

"It's actually fairly simple as long as you have access to quality ingredients. You're lucky that Duncan's Market in downtown Sugar Falls has a great Italian section."

"Charlotte. Look at our kitchen. Does this look like the kind of place where we cook up a lot of arugula and Mediterranean olives?"

"First of all, why would you cook olives when you can buy them at the store?" She glanced around at the small enclosed space with the clean but chipped yellow-painted cabinets that had probably been installed during the Kennedy administration. The harvest-gold-colored appliances must've been added during the late seventies, and the linoleum flooring was all but giving up in its efforts to remain white and glued to the corners. "Second of all, this kitchen is what we in the design business call *retro*. And it looks like many wonderful meals were made here."

Alex shoved his hands in his pockets and rocked on the heels of his hiking boots. "Only if you consider

Hungry Man frozen dinners and tater tot hot dish as culinary delights."

Was he embarrassed about his humble upbringing? The last thing she wanted to do was cause the guy any unnecessary shame. Especially in his own home. Her chest constricted. Or maybe he was simply uncomfortable with having a stranger in his kitchen. Although, he hadn't treated her like a stranger back in that tent. Or in her friend's driveway two days ago.

"If it's any consolation, I kind of cheated by doing most of the prep work at Kylie's. I'm mostly just assembling and reheating things here."

"Can I help?" he asked. His nearness wasn't very helpful at all. In fact, it was distracting. But at least he wasn't kicking her out of his house. Not that she wouldn't go politely. She didn't want to be in his home any more than he probably wanted her here. But Kylie and the girls had already arranged everything before she could explain to her friend that spending any additional time with the sexy river guide was a bad idea.

"That's okay. I'm used to working in the kitchen alone."

"Can I offer you something to drink?" He pulled a bottle of Coors Light out of the fridge, but she shook her head.

"I brought some wine if you want to uncork it and let it breathe before we start the appetizers."

He lifted an eyebrow at her and she held her breath, wondering if she'd made yet another assumption—one that involved an outdated kitchen and three bachelors actually owning a working corkscrew. Luckily, he opened a drawer and fumbled through some utensils before pulling one out.

"Did you get your article done?" Alex asked, still making no move to leave.

She nodded as she arranged the antipasto platter. "I emailed it last night so that it could be edited and go live on the website this morning. I mentioned Russell's Sports and provided readers with a link to make rafting reservations. Hopefully, you get a little extra business for all your trouble."

A creak, followed by a thwerp of air sounded as he pulled the cork out of the wine. He set it on the counter and she felt his eyes on her. "You weren't any trouble."

Why was he looking at her like that? As if she were wrapped in prosciutto and he wanted to eat her up. She gulped. "Still. Having all the rescue footage might have given people a bad impression."

"To be honest with you, Dad's been so busy fielding online requests today, he actually let Com take some of the phone calls."

"You don't normally let your grandfather answer the phone?"

"Would you?" Alex took a drink of his beer and she tried not to stare at the way his lips caressed the bottle or how his Adam's apple slowly moved as he swallowed.

Whoa, she thought, the old oven must be preheating pretty quickly because it was stifling in this kitchen. Charlotte wiped her brow with the back of her hand, then adjusted her headband, tempted to throw the useless thing back in her purse. "Would I what?"

"Never mind." His chin tilted down and a little line appeared between his brows. "Are you okay?"

She turned her back to him so she could rinse the

arugula and order her legs to stop wobbling. "I've never been better."

Charlotte Folsom, that's a damn lie. You're lucky your daughters aren't here to catch you fibbing like this.

"Good, because I've never been hungrier."

"It'll be another forty-five minutes or so." Charlotte looked out the window above the sink and spotted an old wooden picnic table on the back porch. The kitchen was too narrow to accommodate any sort of seating arrangement, and when she'd first arrived, she'd noticed the dining table inside the house was covered with stacks of old fishing magazines and a small, deflated raft with a patch kit nearby. Up until that point, she'd wondered where in the world she'd serve their meal. "Should we eat outside?"

"Where?" he asked. She still had her back to him, but could sense him standing just a few inches behind her, looking out the window over her shoulder.

"That table right there?"

"That's where Com cleans his fish."

Charlotte couldn't stop her nose from scrunching. "Then where do you normally eat?"

"Either in town," Alex jerked his thumb toward the living room. "Or in there. With the TV trays."

A wave of pity settled in Charlotte's chest and she tore the leafy greens with a determination she normally reserved for kneading dough. She didn't care how awkward things were between her and the youngest member of the Russell family, she was going to provide these men with a home-cooked meal to remember.

Alex had to pull the linen closet apart, but he finally found the white lace tablecloth Granola used to use for company. Charlotte had asked him to clear off the dining room table, but when she'd sent him on a mission to find something to cover the scarred oak, he'd been at a loss. After two trips outside to consult with his father and to make sure Com wasn't teaching her funny and inquisitive daughters how to track a mountain lion, Alex shook out the delicate old material that hadn't seen fresh air in over twenty-five years.

The dust embedded itself in his throat, making him cough, then swear. It definitely wasn't white anymore, and the lace had more moth holes than flowers.

Why did they have to put on this farce of a dinner party, anyway? If Charlotte wanted them to eat a good meal, couldn't she have just mailed them a gift card to Patrelli's or one of the other restaurants in town? Seeing a female commandeer the sacred, masculine domain of the Russell household seemed almost unnatural—like witnessing a shark swimming down the Sugar River.

Not that Charlotte was a shark—although she was certainly ferocious when it came to her food preparation and staging—but Alex had never so much as brought a date home to meet his family. So having a woman he'd been intimate with bustling around his kitchen playing Holly Homemaker had his gut doing a nose-dive.

She was supposed to go back to her own world, not show up with her fancy recipes and lifestyling ways and make his world seem drab by comparison. Charlotte had already thanked him for saving her life—and her magazine article—then they'd said goodbye. The strings had been cut. Snip, snip.

But Kylie Gregson and his grandfather had taken matters into their own hands and, somehow, he was playing host to the woman and her daughters, trying to pretend that his own family wasn't a bunch of uncivilized hill people.

At least they didn't have any criminals in his family tree. Not that it was Charlotte's fault that her ex-husband was a crook and a con artist. Alex had tried not to delve deeper into her background, but one little internet search yesterday led to dozens of articles about Mitchell Ford's criminal prosecution and ninety-plus-year prison sentence. It also led to a few stories about her wealthy socialite parents, who were out of the country during the scandal and had been wise enough not to invest any of their millions in their son-in-law's financial schemes. According to one of the online tabloids, the guy had so many aliases, Charlotte legally changed her and her daughters' last names back to her maiden one and hadn't been in contact with the jerk since.

At least his mother's abandonment was much less dramatic. As far as he knew. He supposed he should be grateful for that. But the fact remained that his initial instincts about Charlotte coming from money had been spot on.

He shoved the torn lace tablecloth back into the linen closet. It wasn't that he was embarrassed by his upbringing, Alex told himself. It was just that Charlotte was the type of woman who naturally decorated every inch of her surroundings. Like putting those big, fussy bows in her daughters' hair and making them wear fancy dresses and patent leather sandals to a cabin out in the mountains. Clearly, the little girls couldn't wait to ditch those bows and explore the wilds of his backyard. And he couldn't blame them.

Alex's idea of spiffing things up was to scoop his

grandfather's waders and fishing poles off the sofa and shove them into the hall closet. If you didn't count the black ostrich cowboy boots he wore for special occasions, he didn't even own a pair of dress shoes.

She had to be looking down her aristocratic nose at their humble bachelor pad. Like his own mother had probably done all those years ago, when she'd found herself saddled with an unwanted souvenir from the time she'd stepped outside her comfy, ritzy life. Dad never talked about Mariah Judge—what little information Alex had came from Com, who'd never made it a secret that snobs like her had no business leaving the city and imposing their high-maintenance lifestyles on simple country folk like them.

Which was why it was so surprising that his grandfather had taken such a shine to Charlotte Folsom and her daughters. Maybe the old man suspected something had happened between them. Alex had been careful to restock the first aid kit as soon as Scooter and Jonesy and the rest of the rescue crew hauled in their supplies.

But Com had been dropping a lot of hints lately about great-grandchildren and carrying on the Russell family name. When Matt Cooper, the police chief of Sugar Falls, announced that his wife was pregnant, his grandfather made a wisecrack about all of Alex's buddies beating him at a lot more than poker.

Having children and settling down wouldn't normally be considered a competition to most people. But Commodore Russell wasn't the least bit normal. And neither was having Charlotte in his house.

Alex stretched his neck before walking back toward the kitchen. "I don't know how to break this to you, but the tablecloth is pretty much shot."

Charlotte was now wearing an apron she must have found in a kitchen drawer because Alex sincerely doubted she owned one that read "BBQ King," let alone travelled with it. "*The* tablecloth? As in you only have one?"

"How many do we need?"

Turning around, she shook her head as if she couldn't fathom someone not stocking shelves full of table linens. Well, Alex had news for her. Decorating for dinner didn't exactly rank too high up on his list of necessities. But he was too distracted by the way her dress outlined her rear end as she bent over to set a casserole dish in the oven.

The gold-colored metal door squeaked closed, warning him to pull his gaze back up before she caught him staring. She leaned against the counter and asked, "Would you mind if I looked around for something else we could use?"

He gestured out of the kitchen with an open palm. "Make yourself at home."

It was too damn hot in there and Alex didn't like the way his hormones had hijacked his common sense. He needed fresh air and a reality check so he headed outside to check on the girls.

Audrey, the younger one, had lost one of her pink shoes and was flying down the zip line that ran from the tree fort to the other side of the backyard. The little girl didn't talk much, but she was screaming with laughter by the time his dad caught her, and Alex looked toward the kitchen window praying Charlotte hadn't witnessed her daughter go from acting like a teddy bear to a modern-day Tarzan.

"Where's Elsa?" he asked.

Vic tossed the five-year-old onto his shoulder. "She and your grandfather went looking for something."

"Dad, these girls are from the city and their mom probably won't be happy with them doing anything too dangerous." Alex looked at the heavily wooded area behind his home and ran a hand through his hair. "I told him no mountain lion tracking."

Just then, Com and the six-year-old girl came traipsing out of the trees. Elsa was holding something long and twisting above her head. "Check out the snake we found."

A loud shriek came from the house followed by the slap of the back porch screen, then their mom was dashing across their yard in her high-heeled sandals calling out, "Sweetie, put it down. Carefully, please."

Unfortunately, the woman didn't appear to be concerned about her own lack of caution. Alex saw the gopher hole a split second before Charlotte's foot found it and he was already running to her as she went down. Both girls came sprinting to their mother's side, dual looks of concern marring their cute faces.

"Are you okay, Mommy?" Elsa asked, still holding her slithery friend.

"I'm fine. I just jarred my ankle a little bit." The ankle in question was already swelling and Alex recognized the brave determination on her face as Charlotte tried to stand up. She wobbled, and he immediately wrapped his arm around her waist, causing his muscles to tense. Hell, even with her injured and a yard full of witnesses, his body still reacted to touching her.

Audrey didn't say anything, but nudged Vic forward. "The little one is right," Vic said, despite the fact that Alex hadn't heard the small girl utter a word. "I should probably carry you inside."

"Watch out," Commodore pushed his son out of the way and puffed out his barrel chest. "I'll carry her."

"No, no. That's not necessary," Charlotte said. "I can walk just fine."

Her proud smile slowly crumpled with each step she hobbled, and she'd only made it a few feet when Alex couldn't take seeing her in any more pain and swept her up into his arms.

She let out an *oomph* of air and stiffened her body. Her eyes were now violet, filled with pain and only a few inches from his as she looked at him intently. "No, really. I'm okay. I can walk."

"Charlotte, just relax," he said under his breath, trying not to make this into a bigger scene.

She brought her face closer to him and he felt her warm breath as she whispered in his ear. "I don't want the girls to think I'm hurt. They'll worry."

"But you *are* hurt."

"Not that badly."

"I get that you want to protect your daughters. However, it will be a lot worse if I let you put any more pressure on that swelling ankle." He could feel the second his words dawned on her because she let her muscles relax and finally settled in against him.

But in his haste to lift her, he hadn't taken the time to ensure that her dress didn't flutter up and he was surprised to find his palm on the bare skin of her outer thigh. A breeze caused the hem to tickle the back of his hand and he felt her jerk the fabric over them both.

Her eyes grew wide, and a deeper shade of purple, as if she'd just now realized how intimately he was touching her. But then a voice reminded him that they had an audience.

"You wanna hold Prince String Bean, Mommy?" Elsa asked from behind them. "He might make you feel better."

Charlotte's straight hair brushed against his cheek, making him long for the messy curls, as she turned back toward her daughter. "Who's Prince String Bean?"

"My new pet snake."

Charlotte released her hold on his shoulders and he could imagine her pointing one of those long pretty fingers at her daughter. "Elsa Montgomery Folsom, you put that thing down right this second."

"Mr. Commodore says it's not poisonous, Mommy."

"I also said that garter snakes belong outside and not as pets." *Huh.* Com's voice was way gentler than it had ever been when Alex was a boy and brought home everything from a baby raccoon to a western toad.

"But I wanna keep him," Elsa sniffed.

His grandfather knelt down to deliver a kinder version of the lecture Alex was all too familiar with, while he carried Charlotte inside. He set her down on the worn brown-plaid recliner, which was normally reserved for only Com. But since the old man and his impromptu snake hunt were the indirect reason for their guest's injury, his grandfather would have to find somewhere else to sit.

"Audrey says what you need is a good cuddle from a teddy bear." Vic spoke up.

Alex squinted at the five-year-old balanced on his dad's right hip. He hadn't heard her say that at all. But when Charlotte opened her arms and the small child moved onto her lap, he had the bizarre thought that the girl and his father were somehow communicating in other ways.

The timer pinged on the oven and Charlotte tried to stand up. Alex reached down, grabbed the side handle on the recliner and extended the footrest, preventing her from going anywhere.

"Oh, cool," Elsa said as she came inside with Com, thankfully without Prince String Bean. "It's a magical chair that turns into a bed. Does this one do it, too?"

Vic chuckled as he went into the kitchen. The older girl hopped onto the faded turquoise recliner that was next to her mom's and played with the handle like a kid with a new jack-in-the-box toy, shrieking in delight every time the footrest popped out. Com looked at both of the occupied chairs before letting out a loud huff and plopping his old body on the brown striped sofa—the least used item of furniture in the house besides the dining room table.

Alex had never thought of his house as being anything other than a place to sleep and stow his gear. The cabin was comfortable and suited their needs, and he'd never wanted anything more than that. It hadn't been remodeled or refurnished since Granola passed away, and if his mother had thought the place wasn't good enough way back then, he could only imagine what someone like Charlotte must think of it. Although, her exuberant daughters seemed enthralled by the most ordinary things.

"Mommy, can we get one of these magic chairs when we get home?" Elsa asked.

"I don't know where we would put it, sweetie," Charlotte said absently, as she stroked her other child's hair, hopefully not noticing the missing bow.

Vic returned to the living room with an ice pack, making Alex feel even more useless. He took it from his dad and placed it on Charlotte's swollen ankle, then asked, "What do you need me to finish in the kitchen?"

"I can do it." Her arm stiffened and she tried to push herself up. This time, he put his hand on her shoulder. "Everything's almost done, anyway."

"No, Charlotte. You're our guest and you need to keep that thing elevated." Her muscles tensed under his fingers and Alex got the impression that most people didn't tell her no. "In fact, I should probably take you back to Shadowview for X-rays."

She blasted him with a cool look and pursed her lips before giving her regal head one subtle shake. Yeah, the woman definitely had a thing about hospitals. But his threat had the desired effect and she sighed. "The dressing needs to go on the salad, then top it with the grated parmesan."

She continued to give him detailed instructions about each dish, and he saw her eyes grow round when Vic began opening up the TV trays and setting them around the living room. "I...uh...thought we could eat in there." Charlotte gave a pointed look at the dining table, which she'd covered with a faded quilt and set with the Corningware plates Granola used to keep in the china cabinet—back when they used the thing for dishes and not as a drying rack to hang damp wetsuits.

Seeing how prettily she'd set the table with what few options they'd had available made the rest of their cabin look crude by comparison, and the knot of shame that had been threatening to choke him all evening finally was more than he could swallow. How had his grandfather and his dad let things get so bad?

"Why's my momma's birthing quilt out here?" Com asked the room in general.

Elsa froze, mid-recline, her hazel eyes glued to the older man. "You have a mom?"

"'Course I do. Even wild animals have mommas. She gave birth to me right on that there quilt, in fact."

Alex squeezed his eyes shut, but not before he saw Charlotte's cheeks turn the same color as her swollen ankle. "I'm sorry," she said. "I didn't know that was an heirloom. I just thought it was pretty and would make a lovely tablecloth."

"Don't think nothin' of it." Com waved his hand. "Momma used to set a pretty table, too."

Elsa climbed off the La-Z-Boy and walked over to study his grandfather's weathered face, trailing a finger down one of his wrinkles. "Is your mommy still alive? 'Cause, if so, she must be a hundred years old."

Com hooted with laughter, Alex bit back a grin and Charlotte looked as if she wanted to sink into the brown plaid fabric. "Nah, she passed away a long time ago. But she was a tough old bird. She would've liked a fun sassbucket like you."

"Sassbucket," the little girl repeated, then broke into a fit of giggles. Com began tickling her and Audrey leaped off her mom's lap to get in on the playful action.

Charlotte's lips relaxed into a smile, and Vic shouted words of encouragement to the two girls. A dampness spread across Alex's palms and he shoved his hands into his pockets. This whole scene was way too cozy. Too family-like. When he was at his friends' houses and witnessed how they interacted with their wives and kids and extended relatives, he'd always been fine with it. He'd never felt envious or like he was missing out. But now that it was happening in his own home, with his own family, he didn't quite know what to feel. All he knew was that whatever this feeling was, he needed to get the woman—and all the homey possibilities she invoked—out of his life before he started liking it too much.

And wanting something he knew he could never have.

Chapter Seven

After dinner, Alex drove her and the girls home in Kylie's SUV, while his father followed in one of the Jeeps. Her daughters were passed out asleep in the backseat, and as they pulled into the Gregsons' driveway, Charlotte was reminded of the last time he'd dropped her off here.

When he shut off the engine and the interior lights dimmed, she wondered if he would kiss her again. Instead, he pointed to her ankle. "You promise to have Garrett McCormick check on it first thing in the morning?"

"Who?"

"My friend, Dr. McCormick. He's an orthopedic surgeon—one of the best. Even if it's just a sprain, you should still get it checked out."

"Will he mind doing a house call?" she asked. Because the last thing Charlotte wanted to deal with was going back to a hospital, with or without her girls in tow.

But before Alex could respond, Kylie Gregson came out her front door, not looking the least bit sick. Maybe it had been one of those twelve hour bugs. Or maybe her friend didn't want the Russells over to her house, after all. Something prickled along the back of Charlotte's neck and she had to tell herself that she was overthinking things. After all, Kylie had been the one to suggest, then orchestrate the thank-you dinner. Besides, Charlotte didn't have time to wonder about anyone's motives before the redhead jerked the passenger door open, a worried expression across her brow.

"Commodore called and said you were on your way home with a busted ankle." Her friend's voice was loud with concern, causing the six-year-old in the backseat to stir awake.

"Hey, Aunt Kylie," Elsa said, her eyes popping open as if she hadn't been sound asleep just a second ago. "You missed out on the bestest time, ever. They had these magic chairs that turn into beds and these teeny-tiny tables for just one person and we watched a fishing show on their ginormous TV and I found a snake named Prince String Bean and Mr. Russell Number Three said a bad word and then he lifted Mommy right up in his arms like the Woodsman carried Snow White after she woked up from eating the poisoned apple."

"Well," Kylie replied, laughter blossoming behind her eyes. "I don't know which one of those exciting things to address first, but I'm pretty sure it wasn't the Woodsman who kissed Snow White. Or if there's even a Woodsman in the story."

Charlotte heard her friend's dramatic emphasis on the word *kissed* and prayed that Alex hadn't noticed.

"But Mr. Russell Number Three lives in the woods and his house is so neat," Elsa said, climbing out of the car and taking Kylie's hand. "Also, Mr. Commodore—who's really Mr. Russell Number One, but we call him Mr. Commodore for short—said my mom makes the best noodle bake he's ever tasted and he called me Dumpling and a sassbucket and said we can come back to visit anytime we want."

Audrey, despite the lively chatter, was still asleep when Vic made his way to the rear door and lifted her up out of her booster seat. Which meant that unless Charlotte could pull herself out of the car and limp up to the porch, Alex would be carrying her again.

She was pretty sure nothing was broken, but as she scrambled to climb out of the passenger side, Charlotte bumped her injury against the steel doorjamb and had to bite her lip to keep from yelping out in pain.

Too late. Alex was already by her side, witnessing her scrunched-up face and giving her a reprimanding look.

"You do kind of look like Snow White with that headband in your hair," he said, before effortlessly lifting her up into his arms. This time, though, Charlotte carefully kept the skirt of her dress tucked around her legs. She could still feel the imprint of his hand against her bare thigh from two hours ago and, as they passed through the front door, she thought about purposely banging her ankle against the wood frame just so that she'd have a different feeling to take her mind off of the intimate memory. But she resisted the temptation only because she didn't want her more-than-likely sprain to turn into a broken bone.

As the procession moved into the entryway, Vic almost crashed into Elsa when she stopped midsentence to lift up the hem of her dress and proudly show Kylie the tear she'd gotten from a rusty nail sticking out of the ladder in Alex's old tree fort. Maybe when the doctor came to check Charlotte's ankle in the morning, she should ask about the necessity of getting her daughter a tetanus shot.

As they stood there waiting for the others to resume their pace, Alex shifted his hold on her. The movement brought her closer against him and her startled gasp was loud enough to bring his full attention to her face.

Having his eyes, his lips, that close to hers, made her draw in another mouthful of air.

"Are you okay?" Alex asked.

"Of course. It's just that this house is so pretty, it still takes my breath away every time I come in the door."

She tried to tell herself that it wasn't a complete lie. The Gregsons' home was effortlessly luxurious, but relaxing at the same time. Really, it should be featured in a magazine spread about lakeshore vacation homes, and Charlotte had suggested as much to her hosts. However, Drew, being the complete opposite of his wife in terms of showmanship, worried his patients would view him as unrelatable.

Personally, she thought every human could relate to such a peaceful and comfortable house. The custom-designed gourmet kitchen was a waste, given Kylie's lack of culinary talent, but it looked out onto the open floor plan of the great room with its tall wood-beamed ceiling, river rock fireplace and a wall of windows framing a perfect view of Lake Rush.

"Compared to this place, you must think I live in a dump," Alex said, before giving a self-deprecating laugh.

When Charlotte had been a little girl, one of their cleaning ladies used to bring her son to work with her whenever the kid's grandmother was too sick to babysit him. Charlotte, desperate for someone her age to talk to, tried to befriend the boy, but he'd laughed in that same way and said rich people were boring and lived in boring houses. The memory caused her to stiffen in Alex's arms.

She'd been on the receiving end of reverse snobbery too many times not to recognize it now. Or to be bothered by it. By her third year of marriage, Charlotte had finally come to the conclusion that no matter how warm and welcoming she was, she couldn't make someone like her. Or love her.

She should've just let the remark pass. After all, who cared what conclusion Alex had mistakenly assumed about her? It wasn't like she was ever going to see the man again. Yet the thought of him feeling inferior because of something she couldn't help made her rib cage feel all crumbly—like the topping of a fruit cobbler.

"Actually," she said, "I think your house has a ton of character and charm. The girls and I both felt right at home there."

"Yeah, right." Alex rolled his eyes before setting her on the oversized L-shaped sofa. "Think Kylie would get pissed if I bought Drew a magic reclining chair like Com's for his birthday?"

"You can ask her when she and your dad come back

from putting the girls in the guest bedroom." Though she was positive that her stylish friend would object to that particular gift, Charlotte was proud that she'd diplomatically avoided answering the question while at the same time warning them both that witnesses would be returning soon.

"I'll grab you an ice pack," he said, before going into the kitchen to rummage around in the freezer. For a man who'd been so quick to scoff at their plush surroundings, Alex certainly knew his way around this house and moved around the place as comfortably as if he were in a tent in the woods. Then again, Alex was also good friends with the Gregsons and had probably spent more time here as a guest than Charlotte. The realization confirmed that his initial comment was a dig at her and not the actual house itself. The crumbly feeling intensified.

When he returned, Alex's fingers were gentle as he arranged her foot on a pillow propped up on the overstuffed ottoman, and Charlotte, falling under the spell of his touch, almost forgot about his snide accusation. But when the obvious sound of steps echoed from the hallway, he pulled his hands back as though her skin was covered in lava rather than an ice-filled baggie.

"You ready to go, Dad?" he asked Vic, then scrubbed his hand over his face, as though he could wipe off his eagerness to get away from this house and away from her.

"Sure," the middle-aged Russell replied before looking down at her. "Audrey said to tell you good night."

The nonexistent lava made its way to Charlotte's heart. Audrey didn't really talk to anyone, leaving her mom and sister to pick up on the girl's nonverbal cues.

Yet there seemed to be an immediate bond between her quiet daughter and Alex's father. Seeing both of the girls interact with the Russell men tonight had already been a bittersweet indication that they didn't have any sort of strong male role model in their lives. But witnessing the way Vic easily communicated with her child caused a ripple of regret to boil up in her chest. It wasn't like Audrey would ever see the caring and intuitive man again. Just like Charlotte wouldn't see his son again.

Luckily, Charlotte was used to saying goodbye and being on her own. She'd never wanted the same lonely existence for her daughters, which was why it was a good thing they were leaving before anyone got too attached.

"Thank you again for driving me and the girls back. Good luck with the upcoming whitewater rafting season." She spoke to both of the Russell men; however, she could only bear to look one of them in the eyes.

As soon as they left, Kylie grabbed a pint of ice cream and two spoons, then plopped down beside Charlotte on the sofa.

"I'm happily married," Kylie said, pointing a scoop of mint chip at the front door. "But I'm not afraid to say that that is one good-looking man."

Charlotte felt heat flood her cheeks. "I guess, if you like the macho, outdoor type. But he can be a little standoffish."

"You thought Vic was standoffish?" Kylie looked incredulous and Charlotte immediately realized her mistake. She'd forgotten about the "hunkiest" reference of a few days ago, but her friend at least pretended not to notice by continuing. "I think Mr. Russell Number

Two—as Elsa calls him—is an absolute sweetheart. I swear, half the women in Sugar Falls have a crush on Alex's dad, and I'd bet most of their female clientele request him by name."

Charlotte bit her lip before asking, "Do you think they ask for Alex by name, too?"

"Probably. But Alex isn't real big on socializing with the customers from what I understand."

Charlotte choked on a bite of ice cream. Instead of patting her on the back, her friend zeroed in.

"Spill it, Miss Bay Area," Kylie said, referring to Charlotte by her last pageant title.

"Spill what?"

"Don't give me that. What happened between you and Alex?"

"I made dinner, then I sprained my ankle when I was running around in his yard like a lunatic thinking my daughter was going to get bit by a poisonous snake."

"And?"

"And then he had to carry me. Hey, I thought you were sick."

"I am." Kylie attempted a fake cough.

"With a stomach bug?"

"Are we talking about me or are we talking about the way you and your sexy woodsman couldn't take your eyes off each other?"

"I'd prefer to talk about you." Charlotte looked at the disappearing pint between them because it was easier than meeting her friend's knowing expression.

"I can wait all night if you want." Kylie settled back into the cushions. "But if history repeats itself, Audrey is going to be down here in about an hour wanting a glass of water. Then my twins will wake up at midnight for their feeding and Elsa will be sleepwalking to the bathroom at two. This is our only chance to have a conversation uninterrupted by kids, so unless you want an audience, you better start talking."

Charlotte sighed then, bit by bit, told her friend about the night she'd spent with Alex by the river, leaving out the more personal details. "It was supposed to be a no strings attached kind of thing, but I've never had a one-night stand, let alone had to see the guy after the fact."

"Sugar Falls is a small town," Kylie said, stretching. Even with her saint of a husband helping out around the house, the poor woman had to be exhausted having to entertain visitors—two of whom were additional children. Charlotte hoped they hadn't already overstayed their welcome. "It would've been hard *not* to run into him. If you would have told me sooner that seeing him again would be so uncomfortable, I never would have suggested you make them dinner."

"As your guest, I could never be so ill-mannered as to suggest who you should invite to your house."

"That's why you always won Miss Hospitality," her friend sighed. "Now I feel like a crummy host for orchestrating the whole…I mean, accidentally putting you in that position."

"It's not that I'm uncomfortable around Alex, it's just that…" Charlotte paused, unable to put her feelings into words. She had always been good at making others feel at ease, but had never quite mastered that trick for herself.

"Do you still like him?" Kylie asked.

"Of course I like him. He's very thoughtful and

kind. And he and his family were so sweet with the girls. You should've seen how Vic and Audrey can talk without even speaking and how Commodore patiently answered every single one of Elsa's questions about animals and trails and living off the land. I had no idea she was so fascinated with all that stuff."

"I don't think I've ever heard someone refer to Commodore Russell as patient, but all the Russell men have a way with kids. I was just telling Drew that it's a shame Alex doesn't have any of his own."

Charlotte looked sideways at her friend. "He gave me the impression he wasn't the type to settle down."

"He gives everyone that impression. Drew thinks it's some sort of defense mechanism, but then again, my husband is a therapist and has some fancy psych term for everything. So, what are you going to do if you run into him again while you're in town?"

"I doubt that'll happen. It was tough enough saying goodbye to the guy. Twice, I might add. But since the girls and I are planning on leaving tomorrow, there shouldn't be any more awkwardness."

So maybe Charlotte had spoken too soon about leaving the following day, because when Dr. McCormick took an X-ray and examined her sprain, he fitted her with a splint and recommended she limit any excessive activity, including driving and airline flights, for the next few days. Sure, she could've dealt with a little extra pain and swelling and flown home anyway, but as Kylie reminded her, once she was back in San Francisco, who would help Charlotte with the girls if she was on crutches?

So she gave in and rescheduled her flight for the following week. But by Friday morning, her ankle was almost back to normal and Charlotte was going so stir-crazy that she asked Kylie if they could go out to breakfast and spend the day in town checking out the antiques stores and quaint shops on Snowflake Boulevard.

As they exited Kylie's SUV in front of the Cowgirl Up Café, Audrey and Elsa—who were also suffering from cabin fever—began shoving at each other in their quest to get to be the one who got to push Kylie's twins in the double stroller, and Charlotte thought she might have to use one of her crutches to separate the two. Instead, she told them to hold still while she clipped Audrey's curly hair back and wiped a spot of dried toothpaste off Elsa's cheek.

The girls needed to start their summer schedules of art classes, ballet and enrichment studies, because sitting around at Kylie's house all week after sampling a taste of the great outdoors at the Russells' cabin had everyone ready to explode. And just because Audrey was pretending to be a fishing pole today didn't make her any less hot-tempered—especially when she was using her arm as the line and her hand as the hook to snare her sister's braid.

Charlotte wedged herself between the two little girls. "We are going into a public place and you will act like the proper ladies that I raised you to be."

Both of her daughter's eyes grew wide at her raised tone and Charlotte clamped her lips shut when she realized her voice had sounded just like her own mother's.

On the rare occasions Carmichael and Lila Folsom had deigned to collect their only progeny from the nanny or the boarding school in order to show her off to their friends and business associates, Charlotte had been the recipient of the same warning. A wave of shame washed through her and she immediately pulled each girl in for a kiss. "Sorry for sounding so mean. Mommy just gets cranky when I haven't had any waffles in a long time."

"But Uncle Drew made us some on Tuesday," Elsa said, still enthralled with the concept of ready-made frozen food items that could go in a toaster.

"I think your mom meant homemade ones," Kylie said, trying to shove her extra-wide stroller through an entrance painted to look like swinging saloon doors. It was a good thing Kylie's husband was somewhat knowledgeable in the kitchen, because if her friend had been in charge of cooking this week, they would've been living on takeout and Eggos.

The smell of bacon and coffee immediately lifted Charlotte's mood and she hoped this restaurant lived up to its hype of home-style meals. It certainly lived up to its name, with all the sparkly and sequined painted country-themed décor. Who knew saddles could be covered in fuchsia glitter paint and turned into ceiling fans? Or that lassoing ropes could be dyed purple and used to spell out greetings on the turquoise wall? But somehow, the Western-style pictures and cow-print accents made it all work. The cafe was fun and down-to-earth at the same time. Just like the lively older woman Kylie introduced to her as the owner and sometimes waitress.

Freckles' smile was almost as bright as her snug, lime green T-shirt, which didn't exactly match her teased orange hair. The deeply grooved lines around the woman's heavily made-up face suggested a long life well lived with lots of laughter. She continued to shake Charlotte's hand for another thirty seconds. "I've read all your articles, darlin', and just about died when I heard Kylie was bringin' you to town for a visit."

"It's a pleasure to meet you," Charlotte replied. "I'm looking forward to one of your famous biscuits I've been hearing so much about."

"Just wait 'til you get a taste of my huckleberry jam. It's my own recipe and I'm thinking about jarring it up and selling it online. Maybe you can get a picture of it for your next article. Hey, Kip," the woman hollered—quite loudly—to someone back in the kitchen. "Charlotte Folsom is here and wants some biscuits. Put a fresh tray in the oven."

Charlotte resisted the urge to tug at her ear to stop the reverberations ringing inside it. Which was why she must not have heard the little cowbell over the door signaling a new customer. Or rather, two new customers.

Audrey and Elsa made a dash for Alex and Commodore, pulling both of the Russell men toward the hostess stand. Charlotte had just regained her hearing—but had yet to recover from her shock—when Freckles pointed to a group of ladies wearing T-shirts printed with the words *Saucy Wrenches*.

"The Hot Rodettes Car Club is using our bigger booth, but I can push a couple of tables together if y'all want to sit with each other."

Kylie tilted her head, as if to ask Charlotte how she felt about sharing another meal with Mr. No Strings Attached. But with Freckles and the rest of the customers staring in their direction, it wasn't like she could rudely rebuff the men. Before she could decipher Alex's pinched-mouth expression, Elsa and Commodore made the decision for them and were helping a second waitress set up a longer table.

At least she'd been saved the embarrassment of having to sit next to the younger Russell when Audrey reeled him into the seat beside her.

"Where's that handsome daddy of yours, Alex?" Freckles asked.

"He's back at the store scheduling interviews." Commodore answered for his grandson, who looked as if he'd just gulped down a carafe of cold coffee. "Might hafta hire a couple more college kids for the summer."

"Sounds like business is booming," Charlotte said, experiencing a sense of relief that she wasn't the cause of them losing customers.

"It's been picking up." Alex casually shrugged his shoulders. Or perhaps he was just *trying* to be casual. "Actually, Com and I were just grabbing a quick bite to eat before we head back to the store."

Charlotte's ankle, which hadn't been bothering her too much until now, started throbbing in a cadence matching the elevated thumping of her heartbeat. In fact, her pulse had grown so loud, she once again didn't hear the cowbell signaling that someone else had entered the restaurant.

She was so startled at seeing her editor standing inside the little café in Sugar Falls that she almost didn't catch Neal's words. "Well, color me surprised to see the two hottest trends on social media canoodling over an intimate family breakfast."

Chapter Eight

"We're hardly canoodling, Neal." Alex watched as Charlotte laughingly pointed to the distance between their seats across the table, then, being her perfect hostess self, introduced the newcomer.

Although he'd barely had time to pick his gut up off the floor from his surprise at seeing Charlotte again, Alex stood to shake the man's hand. Her boss was everything Alex would never be. Neal Patel dressed like a million bucks, probably had his hair styled for him every morning, and his black shoes were polished to such a shiny finish, Alex saw his own annoyed reflection in them. This was the kind of guy Charlotte was used to and probably preferred. At least, in terms of style and sophistication.

"Who's Shiny Shoes calling a hot trend?" Commodore asked. Alex reached behind Audrey's bobbing head to nudge his grandfather.

Freckles grabbed an extra cow-print-covered cushioned chair and wedged it in between Kylie and Charlotte. For a second, Alex thought the nosy café owner might take a seat, as well. Instead, she rounded up an extra menu and coffee mug for the unexpected guest.

Fielding random phone calls back at their store was suddenly sounding better and better.

"I'm actually glad I caught both of you here," Neal said to him, before leaning closer to Charlotte. "I sent my production assistant over to Russell's Sports and wanted to do a bit of town research myself before talking to you, Lottie."

The apparently familiar nickname rolling easily out of his mouth made the hair on Alex's arms stand up. Not that Alex was jealous of her having romantic feelings for the editor—he'd included the guy in that internet search he'd done last week and found out that Neal was married to a man named Gary—but he was definitely envious of the classy lifestyle the man represented. A lifestyle she was clearly used to, and that he could never provide for her.

"What do you mean, research?" Charlotte asked, her pretty little brow furrowed.

"Have you seen how many online views your article got? And that's just the preview of the three-page spread we have coming out in the print edition," Neal went on excitedly. "The comment section alone has gone viral and everyone has been posting about it on Twitter and Facebook. Glamping! It's ingenious and our readers are dying for a second installment."

Com mumbled something about tourists and a plague of ingrates before shoving a heavily buttered biscuit into his mouth.

"I'm afraid I don't really have enough material for a second article," Charlotte said, before passing the jar of huckleberry jam—which really was picture-worthy—across to his grandfather. "We were only gone twenty-four hours and because it was storming, much of that time was spent inside the te—" She quickly clamped her lips shut.

Her pause spoke louder than the blush staining her cheeks.

"I know." Neal pointed his finger as if to say *ah-ha*. "That's why I'm here. To scout out the possibility of sending you out there again. But this time, the readers are asking about glamping with a family. So since the girls are here with you, I figured what better time?"

"I wanna go glamping." Elsa clapped her hands. "What is it?"

"It's nonsense," Com replied to the little girl before handing her a paper napkin and gesturing toward her nose, which was covered in whipped cream from her hot chocolate. "What you wanna do is go camping. Big difference."

"Okay. I'll go *camping* with you, Mr. Commodore," Elsa volunteered. "You know more about the woods than anyone I've ever met."

Alex doubted Charlotte's adventurous daughter had a long list of acquaintances who were familiar with sleeping outdoors, but she was right when it came to Com's knowledge.

"Wait, hold on." Classy Neal squeezed his eyes shut and steepled his fingers in front of his forehead as if he could channel his thoughts. "I have a brilliant idea. Lottie, you take the girls, and Mr. Russell can take his family, and we can bill the article as a legacy glamping trip."

"No glamping," Alex and Commodore said at the same time. Kylie was covering her mouth with a napkin, her eyes dancing with laughter.

"Fine." Neal waved his well-manicured hand at them. "Camping, glamping, whatever you want to call it. I'm just glad you're all agreeing to the plan."

"Woo-hoo!" Elsa reached out to high five her sister. Audrey responded with a jam-covered smile and her fishing hook hand.

What plan? The one Charlotte's boss pretended to have just pulled out of thin air? The editor seemed too calculating to waste his time coming all the way to Idaho if he didn't have a well-thought out idea to sell.

And when had Alex agreed to anything? He didn't know what to do except sit back and wait for the woman sitting across from him to be the voice of reason and tell her editor that there was no way she was staying in Sugar Falls.

"Wait." Charlotte rubbed at her temples. "When, exactly, are you proposing we do this second camping trip?"

Whoa. What? Alex blinked to keep his eyes from bulging out of his head. Was she seriously considering this?

"As soon as possible," Neal replied. Then he turned to a hovering Freckles to order the corned beef hash and eggs sunny-side up. "Our readers are wanting more and I'd love to have it for the August print issue since it relates to summer activities, but we can do more sneak peeks on our website to get the buzz going early."

"But the Russells haven't even agreed yet," Charlotte pointed out. Thank God someone around here noticed. "And what about the camera crew?"

"What about your ankle?" Alex asked her.

"Hello?" Neal's lofty tone was beginning to grate on Alex's last nerve. "Do you have any idea of how big this will be for your career? I spoke with Debra Braxton over at the Food Network and she said that if this article gets as much attention as the last one, they'd be willing to offer you your own show. And I'm sure Russell's Sports will have to turn down business after this."

"I'd like to turn down *his* business," Commodore mumbled around his toothpick before ordering the supreme sausage omelet.

The fact of the matter was that Alex's family really couldn't afford to turn down any potential customers. They hadn't been able to afford it last summer, either, when Com "accidentally" cancelled the reservations for the staff development department of a mortgage company right after he told a professional hockey team that since they'd lost the Stanley Cup, they could lose the number to Russell's Sports, as well. Sure, there'd been an upswing in reservations this week, but that wouldn't carry them over into next summer. And they really needed the promise of a strong second season to get them into the black.

But would sending his emotions into the equivalent of a Class V rapid by spending another few days with Charlotte in a tent be worth it in the long run? Alex already felt himself being sucked in by her natural current and he should be paddling for the shore, not racing for the falls.

"Are those cinnamon rolls homemade?" Neal asked Freckles, pointing to the bakery case. "I'm going to need to fly my food critic out here to review some of the local restaurants."

The café owner smiled brightly and Alex knew the man had just shifted any potential argument in his own favor. Once Freckles was on board with something, Alex would never hear the end of it. Unless he started making his own breakfasts at home.

Still, he wanted to scream that this was the absolute worst idea in the history of worst ideas—at least, from a personal standpoint, not a business one. But his mouth refused to say the words. His heart refused to be the bad guy. Also, Audrey was pointing to the menu and he was too busy ordering her French toast and a side of bacon for her to say anything else.

Alex had tried to create distance between him and Charlotte, to cut things off and send her back to San Francisco with their night together as a fond memory. As the guy who could handle a casual romantic relationship and not come off as being overly invested. He had a feeling that anything that he said right now wouldn't sound laid-back at all. It was bad enough that they continued to run into each other like this, but forcing them to relive their adventure in the wilderness would be too much. Having their respective families there to witness the spectacle would be borderline insane.

He ordered the lumberjack breakfast and waited for Commodore to tell off Classy Neal—to do his dirty work for him. If his grandfather didn't speak up soon, Alex would wind up offering to drive Charlotte and her adorably sassy daughters back to California himself. Whatever it took to get the woman out of his life sooner.

Instead, Com asked Neal, "You ain't comin' with us, right?"

"Oh, no." Neal shook his head, but not a strand of his perfectly styled black hair moved. "I don't sleep outdoors."

"Good," Commodore said before snagging another biscuit out of the basket in the center of the table. "A city boy like you would only get in our way."

Alex slouched down so low in his seat, he didn't know how he would make it out of this restaurant, let alone out of this mess.

"I can't believe you two are seriously on board with this fiasco." Alex's hands were on his hips as he stared at his dad and grandfather. It was a few days after Classy Neal had that phony epiphany at the Cowgirl Up Café and tried to sell everyone on that ridiculous legacy glamping trip idea. He had less than forty-eight hours to convince himself—and the rest of the town of Sugar Falls—not to buy into the pretense.

"The publicity wouldn't hurt us," Vic replied. "And Mayor Johnston said the Chamber of Commerce thought it might boost tourism."

"Got too much tourism 'round here, if you ask me," Com said, pointing out the window at the occupied parking spaces in front of Auntie's Antiques. "But I did promise Elsa I'd teach her how to fish. Don't you like Miss Folsom's daughters?"

"Of course I like them," Alex said, scrubbing at his freshly shaved jaw. He'd seen the preview of Charlotte's article online and vowed to never grow a centimeter of scruff again. He looked like a homeless lumberjack in one of the photos, although the comments section had blown up with questions about his modeling fees and his relation to Hugh Jackman. "They're little daredevils and funny as can be. Even you like them, Com, which is saying something for an old, crotchety relic like you. But don't you think we're getting a little too chummy with the Folsom family?"

"We're friends with a lot of the families around here," Vic said, then looked at Commodore, who was writing down the out-of-state license plate number of one of Mrs. Cromartie's antiquing customers who'd parked their vehicle on this side of the lot. Last time that happened, the turf war between his grandfather and their neighbor had escalated into threats involving jackhammers and restraining orders, respectively. "Well, some of us are."

"But Charlotte's not from around here." Why did it feel like Alex was talking to a couple of pine trees? "What's going to happen when they leave and go back to their world?"

"Classy Neal can go back to whatever world *he* came from." Commodore didn't bother looking up from his notepad. Why couldn't the old man realize that Charlotte and her boss were two oars on the same boat? Especially after one of the assistants from *Fine Tastes* stopped by earlier today to see their tent inventory so that he could coordinate matching sleeping bags.

"Is something bothering you, son?" Vic asked, and the throbbing in Alex's temples intensified. Normally, his father was about as attuned to human emotions as he was to the stock market. One time, when Alex was in seventh grade, his dad invited one of the biggest bullies at Sugar Falls Middle School to go mountain biking with them. Where was Vic's sense of his son's discomfort when Chuck Marconi was chasing Alex on his Schwinn down the rocky trail? Or ninth grade, when Alex spent fifth period in the nurse's office with a swollen hand from punching that locker after Chuck had thought it would be hysterical to do his book report on *Our Natural Souls* by Mariah Judge during freshman English?

Now, all of a sudden, his dad had apparently decided to pick *this* week to turn into Dr. Phil.

"What do you mean?" Alex turned toward the round rack holding various sizes of life vests and began sorting them so all the red ones were together with the oranges hanging behind.

"Because yesterday you organized that same rack based on prices and today you're trying to recreate the rainbow." His dad's observation made Alex clench his jaw. This was what happened when he allowed Charlotte and her silly lifestyle blogs and articles to put ridiculous decorating notions into his head. "Plus, you haven't quite been yourself since you got back from that rafting trip with Ms. Folsom."

"Nothing happened." Alex's voice was laced with defensiveness, but his dad's face was devoid of judgment.

"Listen, I know where you're coming from." Obviously his dad understood what it was like to fall for a paying customer who wasn't interested in anything other than a brief fling in the wilds of Idaho, but that didn't mean anyone wanted to rehash the past. His entire life, they'd avoided this exact conversation and Alex wasn't about to sit through an awkward speech about making the same mistake his old man had.

Vic scooted his backside onto a nearby shelf holding batting helmets as though he was settling in for long lecture, and Alex's stomach felt like one of the deflated rafts Com should be trying to patch rather than calling Chief Cooper at the Sugar Falls PD to report illegally parked cars.

So instead of acknowledging his father's uncharacteristic attempt to talk about emotions and women who could twist men inside out, Alex seized on the opportunity to save them both from the uncomfortable conversation and occupy himself by doing something more familiar. Like discussing sporting goods.

"We should move these batting helmets and protective gear over to the uniform section," Alex said, needing to change the subject. "I mean, why are we displaying the baseball equipment near the water gear? From a merchandising standpoint, having it here makes zero sense."

And neither did his sudden obsession with product placement. Ugh. He was even using Charlotte's lingo now. But at least it was better than admitting his attraction to the lady. Or having his dad and Commodore give him grief about the dangers of getting too cozy with a woman who would inevitably leave him and return to the city.

Unfortunately, Vic, who was usually so easygoing he'd never pushed Alex to eat his vegetables or Commodore to pay his taxes, was like a dog with a bone when it came to Classy Neal's stupid idea.

"Your grandfather and I would be willing to take the Folsom ladies on the camping trip by ourselves, but the editor from *Fine Tastes* made it clear that the magazine would prefer to have you along as…" His father looked toward Com. "What did he call Alex, Dad?"

Commodore made a scoffing noise. "Eye candy. Though I'm plenty sweeter than the both of you combined."

"Yeah, right," Alex said, then shook his head. "I don't think any sane human has ever referred to you as being sweet."

Vic's laughter and their familiar teasing helped ease the seriousness of the uncomfortable chat, as well as some of the tension Alex had been holding in his jaw.

His grandfather took his toothpick out of his mouth and pointed it at them both. "Miss Folsom thinks I'm sweet and I don't see her daughters complaining none."

"Yeah, well, the jury is still out on their sanity," Alex said under his breath. Actually, Audrey and Elsa were about as normal as any other child on one of his sports teams or in their summer day camps. The girls were perhaps a bit on the quirky side but that's because they were smart and had great imaginations. And their mother loved them like crazy, even if she did tend to dress them in girly clothes they hated and cut their French toast for them when they clearly wanted to use Com's steak knife and do it themselves.

But any female who could wrap a cranky know-it-all like Commodore Russell around her little finger must be from another planet.

"So, are you coming with us, son?" Vic asked, causing Alex's stomach to turn inside out. As much as he hated to admit it—even to himself—he couldn't stand the thought of his dad and grandfather getting to be the only ones who got to spend time with the Folsoms before they left. This time for good.

"As long as you don't invite Chuck Marconi this time," Alex mumbled, mostly to himself.

"What's that?" his dad asked from behind the rack of life vests that he was putting back in order of size.

"Never mind," Alex said, knowing his resolve had slipped before they'd even left the Cowgirl Up Café the other day. "Fine. We'll do the camping trip. But no professional photographers."

"Classy Neal is gonna hate that." Com clapped his hands together gleefully. "I'll call him right now and negotiate our terms."

Vic beat his father to the phone. "No more negotiating for you, Dad. We don't need to be threatened with another lawsuit."

Alex knew the stipulation was unreasonable, but if he was going to re-create what they'd had in the first article—which was what the magazine claimed they wanted—he would only be able to do so authentically if they were in a natural, unstaged environment and Charlotte wasn't in professional mode. Plus, he didn't need any extra witnesses around to see how deeply she'd gotten under his skin.

"Rule number one," Charlotte told her daughters almost a week later, making sure she looked each girl in the eye and had her full attention, "is to listen to the grownups at *all* times."

"We will," Elsa squealed in excitement, and Audrey barely nodded before they raced across the ranger station parking lot to climb into the all-terrain vehicle with Commodore and Vic.

Alex lifted his eyebrow at her. "I thought rule number one was no strings attached?"

Heat infused her cheeks and Charlotte struggled to pretend that she didn't know exactly what he was referencing. She also made a mental note to avoid being alone with Alex the rest of this trip. Her heart and her wobbly knees couldn't take it.

"I think it's too late for them." She nodded toward the foursome. The girls had begged to ride with the older Russell men, which left Charlotte riding in the second ATV with Alex and most of their camping supplies. Originally, Neal had wanted them to re-create the rafting trip, too, but Charlotte decided it was too dangerous for the girls and didn't want to risk some random act of nature stranding them somewhere again.

Alex didn't reply to her observation about it being too late or the fact that she wasn't just talking about their families. Not that anything he could say would make her lingering attraction for him go away. But it was going to be a long two days if they didn't talk to each other at all.

Their destination was a little-known designated camping area outside the national forest and only accessible on foot—which was out because her daughters were too young to hike—on horseback—unfortunately Charlotte couldn't ride—or on one of these hopped-up four-wheelers for adrenaline junkies. As Alex started the engine, she tried not to think of the last time she'd ridden in one of these things with him, or what they'd been doing several hours prior to that ride.

Actually, for nearly a week now, she'd tried not to think about Alex Russell at all. Unsuccessfully. The girls talked about him, as well as his father and grandfather, constantly. Kylie and Drew mentioned him every time she turned around. And readers of the online article had posted more comments about that one picture she'd taken of him standing on the boulder fishing than they had about the gourmet preparation of Trouty or the shots of the gorgeous, green scenery.

The ATV bumped over a fallen branch, jostling her enough that her arm knocked into his. The contact blasted a fissure of heat through her tense muscles, making her skin feel as though it was being flash-fired in a scorching skillet. Prior to their night in the tent, she hadn't been with a man since Mitchell, and she and Alex both knew that their situation was extremely temporary. Charlotte had hoped their first camping trip had been a one-off.

Yet every time she'd seen him since the incident, her mind insisted on recalling every single detail as if it were cataloguing the ingredients of a complicated and decadent dessert recipe. Even when she wasn't in the same room with him, her body ached for him. And now that she sat just inches away from him, every cell positively cried out for his touch.

"So, you've noticed it, too?" Alex asked out of nowhere.

"Noticed what?" Her reaction to him? The way her stomach did its impression of a boiling pot of water every time he was near?

"That my dad and grandpa have gotten pretty attached to your daughters?"

Oh, that. Charlotte had to raise her voice to be heard above the roaring engine. "More like the other way around. I hope Vic and Commodore will let me know if the girls are too much of a bother for them."

"Are you kidding? Dad is one of those quiet types who prefers to privately commune with his surroundings, so Audrey is right up his alley. And Com is in heaven having someone like Elsa asking him every question under the sun. It reaffirms his own belief that he's smart and important."

"I just wouldn't want them to overstay their welcome." Much like Alex probably thought Charlotte was overstaying hers. In fact, she'd never actually gotten the impression she'd been welcome in the first place and she hated the way the perception took her right back to her childhood, triggering those old issues of abandonment and isolation she'd thought she'd overcome.

"Charlotte, they're kids. They're supposed to be curious and adventurous and attention demanding. My family would think it was weird if they were too polite and formal."

Although he'd just complimented her daughters, she tried not to bristle at the implication that *she* was the weird one. "I was raised in a home where children were supposed to be seen and not heard, and I promised myself that when I had my own kids, I wouldn't subject them to the same lonely childhood I had. Unfortunately, old habits die hard. It's difficult not worry about what others think and I hate being an imposition on anyone."

"Do you ever get tired of being so damn polite all the time?" His tone held a note of accusation and she folded her arms across her chest defensively—then quickly grabbed on to a handle when they hit another bump.

"I'm getting tired of it right about now," she mumbled, too low for him to understand over the motor.

"What?" he asked.

She thought about repeating her answer so that he could hear, then remembered that she was better than that. Plus, she knew Alex really wasn't all that keen to take her and the girls camping again. Neal had told her that he complained about all of the magazine's ideas for the theme of the article and then made several stipulations. If only her pride had been on the line, rather than the future of her career, she'd have left Idaho several days ago. So who could blame him for being frustrated with the situation?

Unlike her ex-husband, Alex had been nothing but honest with her from the moment she'd met him. He'd never pretended to be something he wasn't.

This trip was obviously a pain in the neck for him and Charlotte didn't need to exacerbate the tension by appearing unappreciative. She'd learned that lesson in boarding school, when Mitty Bachman had invited everyone from their hall to her bat mitzvah in her hometown of New York City. Charlotte didn't have a way of attending since she was usually stuck at school during the weekends and holidays, but she'd written a nice card and asked her dad's assistant to send a gift.

When all the other girls returned after spring break, they were full of stories about Jasmine Del Re, a snotty eighth grader, who hadn't bothered to RSVP and then showed up with several uninvited friends who'd depleted the candy station and taken extra party favors. Jasmine was never invited to another event outside of school, but Charlotte got to spend that June with the Bachmans in Southampton.

It hadn't cost much to be diplomatic and the reward had meant she wasn't left alone at home all summer with the help.

Society had certain rules and it was easiest to follow them if she wanted to fit in. So, instead of arguing with Alex or saying something that might suggest she didn't appreciate him facilitating this trip at the last minute, Charlotte took her list out of the small pack she'd cinched around her waist and consulted it for the eighth time that morning.

Since they would be gone for two nights this time, she'd brought additional food supplies and kitchen tools. Plus, her last article had addressed living off the land, and this one was supposed to be geared more toward a family excursion so she wanted to concentrate on kid-friendly foods and activities.

When they pulled up to a clearing beside Sugar River, Alex parked behind his father. Vic had already unstrapped the girls from the back seat and Charlotte smiled in relief to see the huge grins on their faces. At least they were enjoying themselves.

Elsa skipped over to them, her brown pigtails bopping in sync with her little pink sneakers. "Mommy, did you see how fast we were going? Did you see when Mr. Vic hit that tree branch and Com almost went flying out? Is this where we're gonna camp? Are there bears here? I wanna see a bear and maybe it will want to sleep in my tent with me if I give it some honey. Did you bring any with us, Mommy?"

Charlotte tried not to shudder at the thought of some huge grizzly eating a lot more than honey. She looked to Alex for help with explaining the dangers of feeding wild animals, but Audrey was already climbing onto his lap, pretending to steer the off-road vehicle.

Maybe they should address childproofing the ATVs and the campsite first.

Alex resecured one of Audrey's braids with a dangling rubber band and Charlotte's heart twisted. No matter how annoyed and inconvenienced he might seem when he was with her, he'd always been nothing but gentle and patient with her daughters. She would have loved to have a father who took the time to notice her hair color, let alone fix it for her.

With Mitchell, Charlotte had been convinced that she could simply instruct him on how to be a caring daddy—as though she were teaching someone how to make a basic frittata. Unfortunately, she'd found out the hard way that paternal instincts weren't something that could be taught. At least, not to anyone who had no desire to learn.

Judging by the way he was now bending down and talking to the girls about the river's current, Alex clearly had both the instinct and the know-how. Nobody would have to teach *him* how to be a dad.

Realizing her improper train of thoughts, she slapped a hand to her head, then winced when the headband dug into her scalp. The pain was a good reminder to her brain that she needed to get her overactive imagination under control. Charlotte had no business thinking about Alex as a quasi father-figure or a quasi anything to her daughters. He'd reiterated that no-strings-attached rule before they'd even driven twenty feet.

Charlotte's insides were wound tight as she unbuckled herself and made her way over to where Vic and Com were unloading supplies. She forced a carefree smile before she spoke. "I had some ideas about how to stage things, but do you guys have a preference for where to put everything?"

Commodore grunted around his toothpick. "My preference is to dump it all right here."

The clearing was long and narrow with about thirty

feet of wild grass between the forest and the rocky shore of the river. The spot was breathtaking, no matter how she looked at it. However, from a photography standpoint, it would make more sense to set the tents up on the eastern-most side of the area. She racked her brain for a way to tactfully propose as much.

"Dad, maybe you should take the girls to collect some wood," Vic suggested, then winked at Charlotte.

Commodore grumbled something about babysitting duty, then called Audrey and Elsa over and told them they were going to have a firewood gathering contest. Charlotte was about to protest that he didn't have to entertain her children but Alex's voice stopped her.

"The old guy won't admit that he tires out more easily nowadays. But trust me, he'd much rather run around with them than haul gear and set up the camp."

"Are you sure?" Charlotte wasn't completely convinced. "I meant it when I said that I didn't want us to be an inconvenience."

"He's sure," Vic spoke up. "Plus, it also keeps my father out of *our* way. He doesn't like to miss an opportunity to remind us that nobody's ever pitched a tent before without his expertise."

"Or caught a fish." Alex smiled at his dad.

"Or built a fire." Vic was using his fingers to count off. "We could keep going if you'd like. But then he'd be back over here before we got done and accuse us of sitting around on our a—butts."

Charlotte laughed. "No, I get it. But later tonight I might like hearing a few stories about growing up with Commodore Russell."

"Then we're going to need a lot of wood for that campfire." Alex quirked his lips at her and her mouth went dry. *Oh, boy.* When that guy smiled, every ounce of decorum that had been drilled into Charlotte floated straight out of her head—along with half the oxygen. She looked around for the Nalgene bottle of water she'd brought with her and told herself it was simply the high altitude that had her so light-headed.

For the next hour, she worked with Alex and his dad to make this little clearing resemble a photo-worthy vacation destination. Every so often, Charlotte would get distracted by the need to call out a warning to Audrey, who now fancied herself to be an off-road vehicle and was racing around revving her make-believe engine, or applying bug spray to Elsa, who had to be told to take the toothpick she got from Commodore out of her mouth before climbing one of the Douglas firs to look for spiders. She was even able to get the older man to wear the floppy-brimmed hat she'd bought him to protect his skin from the sun.

Once everything was set up to her exact specifications, the men joined Commodore and the girls fishing while Charlotte explored the area for things to add to the overall staging of her pictures. This time, the task was easier since she'd brought a professional grade camera with her and the weather was being much more cooperative.

Unfortunately, the camera lens was less accommodating, because it kept finding its way over where the Russell men were teaching her daughters how to catch a fish. And with the click of the shutter, all those thoughts of daddies and daughters came flooding back to her and played war with her heart. For the rest of the day, as she snapped pictures of Alex showing Audrey how to use a net to scoop up a wiggling trout before throwing it back, or of Alex lifting Elsa up onto his shoulders so she could see a bird's nest full of soft blue eggs, Charlotte told herself that nobody would ever see these photos. They were just for her.

When she returned to her life in San Francisco and Alex was nothing but a distant memory, she might look at the images and allow herself to daydream about that time she fell for a guy who would've been perfect for her—and the perfect daddy for her daughters.

If only their lives were different, then maybe that dream could come true…

Chapter Nine

Commodore was already on his second serving of dessert by the time the rest of them had finished their sausage and fennel skillet pizza. Alex had never tasted anything like it in a real kitchen, let alone camping. Although he noticed that Charlotte hadn't eaten a thing because she'd been too busy taking pictures of everything she'd cooked—except the warm cobbler sitting in the Dutch oven, which probably wasn't very photo worthy since a third of it was gone by now.

Granola had had a magnet on her fridge that said, *Today's Menu Choices: Take It or Leave It*—which was still there, holding up a faded and out-of-date baby announcement from Kylie and Drew. But when it came to Charlotte's graceful figure moving around the campsite, he didn't care what she was preparing; he would take anything she dished out and then help himself to seconds.

He'd been the first one to roll his eyes at all the cooking supplies she'd packed, like the collapsible cupboard with built-in cutting boards, the campfire tripod and the open fire swivel grill. While he was amazed at what she'd accomplished with what he'd deemed "unnecessary stuff," he'd be the absolute last one to admit Charlotte had turned this place into an outdoor culinary haven. Besides, he doubted she needed to hear any more praise with the way his dad and grandfather were carrying on.

"A man could sure get used to this kind of cooking," his father said, pointing his not-so-subtle gaze at Alex. Several times today, Vic had busted him staring at Charlotte as she dashed around camp, prepping dinner and dessert, which made Alex question whether the guy was all that oblivious in the human emotions department, after all. "Could you imagine coming home to a meal like this every night, son?"

He shot a cold look at his father. *You said you knew what I was going through. Way to be a team player, Dad.*

"Thank you, Vic," Charlotte said, a glow of pleasure lighting her face.

"Your Granola could field dress a deer like nobody's business," Commodore said, after shoveling the last bit of his cobbler into his mouth. "But she wasn't one for spending much time in the kitchen."

"Who's Granola?" Elsa asked.

"She was my grandmother," Alex replied, the collar of his shirt feeling as though it was getting tighter. "She passed away when I was a little boy."

The six-year-old patted his shoulder. "My grandmother passed away, too."

Charlotte gasped. "No, she didn't, sweetheart."

Her daughter put her hands on her waist. "Then why don't we ever see her?"

"Because she's very busy." Charlotte's reply was so automatic, he wondered how often she'd made the excuse. Especially to herself.

"Do we have a grandpa, too?" Elsa asked, her tone growing suspicious.

"Of course you do," Charlotte said, looking anywhere but at her captive audience.

"Where is he?"

"I...uh... Dubai, maybe?"

Oh, come on. Charlotte's answer had to have sounded as absurd to her as it did to him. Who the hell didn't keep in touch with their daughter and granddaughters on a regular basis? Particularly when they had ones like the Folsom ladies.

Elsa climbed up onto Com's lap. "I would rather have Commodore and Vic be my grandpas."

Charlotte made a choking sound, before turning to dig in the little fanny pack that accented her slim waist—most likely trying to hide her scarlet-tinged cheeks while pretending that she hadn't just heard what her daughter said. Was it wrong for him to hope that the awkward turn in this conversation was affecting her as much as it was him?

"We'd be proud to be your honorary grandpas," his dad said a bit too loudly to Audrey, who was tucked up against Vic. The five-year-old had been doing her rolling log impression an hour ago, but now he guessed that she was possibly pretending to be a speed eating contestant, the way she was putting away food.

The neck of Alex's shirt got even tighter and his

throat filled with enough longing to cut off his airflow. This was getting too cozy again, and he had no idea how to shut it all down. It didn't help that Vic was having no problem casting that relationship net out there on his son's behalf.

"Although, technically," Vic continued, "Com would have to be your *great*-grandpa since he's so much older than me."

"Ain't too old to steal your dessert," Com countered before handing his enamelware plate to a giggling Elsa. "Well, as my honorary great-granddaughter, your first order of business is to fetch us some more of that crustless pie. Or whatever fancy name your mom is calling it."

"I hadn't thought of one for it yet," Charlotte said, while making notes on a little pad as though she were some mad scientist writing out a formula. Alex noted that her face was still a bit too rosy, considering the coolness of the evening mountain air, and her immediate response was a dead giveaway that she'd been listening to this irrational grandparent talk the entire time. "I was thinking of calling it serviceberry crumble."

"Never heard of canned serviceberries before," Commodore said.

"That's because they're not canned," Charlotte explained. "The girls and I picked them this afternoon."

His grandfather made a gagging sound and dramatically grasped at his throat.

"Oh, boy. Are the berries poisonous?" Elsa asked, her wide eyes looking more hopeful than concerned. "Like Snow White's apple?"

Alex had to turn away to hide his smile at the little girl's vivid imagination.

"Of course not," her mom said before leaning over Alex's shoulder and whispering, "Sorry. You're probably wishing for a sleeping potion right about now."

Her breath was warm and tingled the sensitive spot right behind his ear.

"I'm fine," Alex whispered back not feeling fine at all. Having her so close to him, he was surprised his mouth could even form the word. His lungs, which were accustomed to the high altitude, felt as though they couldn't draw in enough air.

"Darn it," Elsa sighed. "I was hoping that if we ate some, the handsome woodsman would hafta kiss us awake."

"I don't think there was a woodsman in that story," Com said. "And if there was, you can just let me go on sleeping 'cause I sure don't wanna get kissed by him."

"What about you, Mommy? Would *you* wanna get kissed by the woodsman?"

Alex settled against the boulder behind him, anxiously awaiting her answer.

"Who wants to make s'mores?" she asked, instead. And her distraction worked like a charm. The girls squealed and sprang up to their feet while Vic shuffled around the campfire looking for some sturdy sticks they could use to roast their marshmallows.

"Not me," Com said, staring off at the mountain ridge where the sun had just set. "Those fresh berries aren't sittin' so well with me. I'm gonna turn in for the night."

His grandfather went searching for his sleeping bag and, after three songs and at least five of Vic's exaggerated stories, Charlotte took a look at her yawning daughters and said it was time for them to go to bed, as well. She and the girls went into the woods to brush their teeth and have some privacy, but when they returned, Elsa asked Alex if he would sleep in their tent. His neck tightened.

"Not tonight, ladies. I brought my own." He looked pointedly at Charlotte, hoping maybe she'd hear the longing in his voice and take pity on him by visiting his tent later tonight.

"But why don't you sleep with Grandpa Vic and Grandpa Com?" The child's use of the honorary titles was like a sucker punch to his gut. "What if a bear tries to get one of them?"

"Are you kidding?" he asked, then forced a laugh. "They both snore so loud, no bear would risk its eardrums to come within a mile of our campsite."

"Tell Mr. Russell good night," Charlotte instructed her daughters, and Alex tried not to show his disappointment at being the only one of his family members addressed so formally. But at least he was no longer being called Mr. Russell Number Three.

The girls both gave him a hug, and little Audrey even gave him a kiss on the cheek. His insides melted like the marshmallow in his s'more and he wasn't entirely sure that he disliked the warm, gooey sensation.

He sent a little salute Charlotte's way before she followed the girls inside the tent. At the sound of the zipper closing them in, he turned and walked back toward the dying fire. His dad had already banked it and Alex saw the lantern light inside the Russells' larger tent.

He stood there looking at the glowing embers of the fire for several minutes before grabbing a flashlight and heading off to the woods to brush his own teeth. He had just started his final check of their campsite perimeter when he saw another lantern coming his way, illuminating the shape of Charlotte's waist and hips, and casting a soft glow up toward her delicate face. His mouth went dry as his pulse sprang into action.

"As soon as the girls closed their eyes, I realized I left my water bottle over here," she said when she stepped into the copse of trees. "Vic said rule number one was try to leave things the way we found them."

"I thought rule number one was always listen to a grownup?" He studied Charlotte soft pink lips. "Or was that rule number two?"

His flirtatious reminder had the desired effect, drawing a blush from her along with the smallest hint of a smile. He was pretty sure his senses would protest if he didn't step closer and touch her. He already knew how good she would smell. How good she would taste. The sound she'd make when his tongue touched hers.

He wasn't sure how long they stood there, staring at each other, but when she set her lantern on the ground, he knew he was done for. Her eyes dragged him in, and right before Alex could tell himself that kissing her would be a bad idea, she reached out and pulled him toward her. His lips clearly remembered what they were supposed to do because the second her mouth opened, heat spread through his entire body.

Like a greenhorn camper who didn't know better, Alex dropped his flashlight onto the bed of pine needles under his feet. One arm encircled her waist to draw her closer and the other hand shaped itself around the nape of her neck, feeling her muscles stretch and contract as her head angled and dipped for more of his kiss.

He would never get enough of her. He might as well relish the heartbreak that was sure to come, because feeling Charlotte's body pressed so fully against his was worth all the emotional fallout he'd have to deal with later. Alex now knew how the poor rainbow trout they'd caught today felt after going for the bait only to find out he'd been hooked. It was just a matter of time before Charlotte would humanely throw him back, as well. But he could no more refuse her than he could stop the rapids.

A sweet moan sounded in her throat and, without releasing the kiss, he walked her a few steps backward so that she was positioned against a sturdy ponderosa. He slid both of his hands down to her hips before lifting her up higher, his arousal centered firmly against the core of her heat. He groaned as she wrapped her legs around his waist, pulling him in tighter.

His fingers were sliding into the waistband of her pants when a flammulated owl in the branch above them hooted, offended by their using its home for their less-than-stealthy reunion.

Charlotte's head whipped back and thunked against the bark of the tree, confusion replacing the desire he'd seen in her eyes just a second ago. He would've taken a step back had her legs not been so firmly tangled around him. Another hoot sounded, along with a mild ruffling of wings.

"It's just an owl," he whispered, planting his hands on her waist to steady her as she regained her footing. He looked up toward the creature, annoyed by the continuing interruption, yet equally thankful that the wise bird had stopped history from repeating itself.

If it hadn't been for some know-it-all nocturnal tree

dweller just a few feet above them, he would've made love to Charlotte again, right here in the middle of a dark forest with their families nearby.

"I'm sorry," he said, then sucked in gulp of air, trying to get his breathing to return to normal. "I never should have done that."

"It wasn't your fault." Her voice sounded formal and way more controlled than his own. "I was the one who started it."

Of course she would be too polite to allow him some well-deserved guilt. Or maybe she just hadn't been as affected by the kiss as he'd been.

"But I took it to the next level," Alex said, trying to read her response. He wanted to emphasize his understanding of their initial agreement, but maybe he could subtly mention whatever feeling this was that he'd thought they shared. "We're supposed to be cutting strings, but every time I look at you this knot between us gets bigger and more complicated, and I worry that we're never going to be able to unravel it."

"Maybe our lives are just meant to be intertwined," she suggested, and he tried not to let the bubble of hope float from his heart to his eyes.

"Someone like you would never be happy living in a small town, occasionally hooking up with some rough-around-the-edges outdoorsman like me."

Several beats passed, followed by Charlotte's mouth forming into a tight line, probably trying to come up with a way to let him down easily. Finally, she said, "That's not true. Sugar Falls is a wonderful town."

Her failure to address the other half of his observation wasn't lost on him. "But…?" he prompted.

"But my job is in San Francisco. The girls' school,

their friends, their art and dance lessons are there. When I was growing up, I vowed that I wouldn't be like my parents. I would always put my family first. I worked too long and too hard for them to have a stable, comfortable home that actually feels like a home and not a coldly decorated museum or a lifeless dorm room. It's why I started blogging and became a lifestyle expert— so that I could create a loving and warm place for them to live. I can't uproot them from everything I've created just because I want to sleep with some guy."

Some guy. The words stung, but at least he now knew that's all he was to her.

Biting back a response that would only embarrass him further, he shoved his hands in his pockets and walked back to the campsite.

Hooking up?

Occasionally?

One minute, Charlotte had been burning up in his arms, the next, her blood was running cold at his description of what would amount to a sex-only relationship. She would've been less insulted if he'd at least suggested they be friends with benefits. Friends? Ha. He hadn't even made an actual invitation for her to move to Sugar Falls. Rather, just a flimsy dismissal of why she wouldn't want to.

A hint of familiarity followed by a flood of shame washed through her when she realized her parents had been training her for this her whole life. To be a trophy child, a trophy wife. And now, Alex was all but suggesting she be a trophy fling—someone who didn't require anyone's personal investment of love or time.

So her response had been an effort to save face and

to explain that she'd never uproot her whole world simply for the occasional night in a tent with Alex Russell. Charlotte deserved more than that. And so did her daughters.

Coming on this camping trip had been an error in judgment. Yet, kissing Alex once again had been a mistake of epic proportions. Unfortunately, before she could maintain a shred of her pride, he walked away from her.

He didn't argue with her, he didn't apologize again, and he definitely didn't declare his undying love for her. Not that she could blame him. Alex'd made it clear from the day they'd met. What was it he kept saying about strings? He didn't want anything tying him down? The problem was, Charlotte was suddenly left feeling like an anchor looking for a ship.

When she returned to her tent, seeing her daughters snug in their bright, cocoon-shaped sleeping bags gave her some comfort. She had these sweet girls; she didn't need Alex or any other man to complete her world. The world she'd made for herself.

Charlotte climbed into her own bed, determined to put the kiss in the woods out of her mind. But instead of falling into a blissful slumber, she fell victim to her own memory and replayed every single moment, every single caress. She tossed and turned, praying the loud shifting of nylon material wouldn't wake anyone else up.

She wanted to blame the owl, who was still out there mocking her, every hoot alluding to the less-than-wise decision to ever get involved with Alex Russell. The sound of the river rushing along over rocks nearby should have helped lure her to sleep. Instead, it made her think of how she'd sunk under the rapids, the rough, churning water disorienting her. Just like when she'd fallen out of the raft two weeks ago, she was now in way over her head.

Charlotte didn't know how or when she finally succumbed to sleep, but both her daughters—as well as a host of birds and forest creatures—started chirping nonstop when the sun came up. Today was Tuesday, and Vic had explained that on Monday evenings, the hydroelectric plant closed off the flow of water from the dam at the north fork of the Sugar River for a twenty-four hour period. Therefore, the water would be calm enough for the girls to go wading and play in the inner tubes Commodore had promised to inflate for them.

Charlotte walked the girls to the designated ladies' area in the woods, and when she passed by the tree that Alex had lifted her up against, she purposely averted her gaze, causing herself to stumble over Audrey, who was pretending to be a pinecone. At least when her daughter had been the teapot, she'd let out a warning whistle.

When they returned to camp, Charlotte saw that Alex's level of avoidance was much stronger than hers because he wouldn't even look in her direction. But at least he wasn't allowing his discomfort with her to affect how he treated her children. He took the girls down to the river and showed them how to use the portable water purifier to refill their plastic bottles, and she had to command her heart not to crumble into a million pieces.

While everyone was occupied, she did what she always did in awkward situations. Or any situation.

She made food. Charlotte whisked up the batter for blueberry pancakes, then poured the first batch into a cast iron skillet. As they were cooking, she cracked eggs into muffin tins and sprinkled them with freshly ground pepper and chives.

"How are you feeling this morning?" she asked Commodore, who was staring at the plump, fresh blueberries she'd brought along as though they were contaminated with deer droppings—which she was now too familiar with, thanks to Elsa's insistence on collecting all things found in nature.

The older man grunted a response, then dug around in one of the storage containers she hadn't packed.

"If you wanna cook with so much fruit, why don't you use these?" He handed her a jar of maraschino cherries.

"Because," Vic said, walking up and taking the jar from his father. "Our bodies would hate us if we filled them with that much food dye at once."

"Some of us just have stronger bodies, I guess," Commodore said, then clamped down more tightly on his toothpick. In the light of day, he wasn't looking much better than he had last night. His normally tan, weathered skin had a grayish tint and his sharp green eyes seemed out of focus.

"If you don't want the berries, I'll make a batch of plain pancakes for you," she offered the older man, whose grimace turned to a half smile as he winked at her.

She found a little enamel pitcher and heated the maple syrup, then laid out a blue gingham tablecloth on the ground so she could stage the breakfast plates. Vic picked up the camera and began taking pictures for her, which allowed her to concentrate on the more important task, which was providing food and comfort.

Sure, writing about recipes and decorating was her job, one she was good at and enjoyed. But preparing these meals outside for her daughters and the Russell men didn't feel like work. It felt like being home in her own kitchen, hosting a small, intimate party for her closest friends.

And feeling like that was dangerous because it wasn't real. Just like her fantasy of Mitchell being the perfect husband and them having the perfect home and family hadn't been real. After two years of marriage, she'd foolishly thought she'd had her life set up the way she'd always wanted it, only to find out her husband had been a complete fraud. His investment schemes, his excuses for missing so many dinners because he was working late at the office, his pleas for forgiveness when he had to make an emergency trip to the Cayman Islands the night Elsa was born—all of it was a farce. No matter how badly Charlotte wanted to design her surroundings, she couldn't allow herself to be blindsided by the truth after it was too late.

Today's truth was that Alex wanted nothing more from her than a one-night stand. Which she'd agreed to initially. But now her building physical attraction to him was playing havoc with her rational thinking and she should've stepped back and looked at the big picture before she saw him standing there in the forest last night in all his sexy woodsman glory.

Charlotte shook her head. Clearly, last night's fairy tale talk was getting to her. She was about to call out for the girls to wash their hands when she noticed Commodore down on a knee, his dry, spotted hand clutched against his chest.

"Com?" She ran to the older man's side, noticing the deep white lines around his mouth. Her fingers were trembling as she placed them on his slumped shoulder. "Are you okay?"

"Just. Heartburn." His words came out in gasps and he tried to wave a hand at her, but his arm couldn't seem to move.

"Here, lie down." As she eased him back against the grass, she felt the dampness of sweat seeping through his flannel shirt. She wanted to yell out for help, but didn't want to alarm anyone. "Let me get Vic and Alex."

"Nah," Com said, his gruff voice barely a whisper. "I'm. Fine."

She could tell by the effort he was making to get each word out that he wasn't fine at all. Luckily, Vic must have seen what was going on and was sprinting across the campsite, her camera bouncing from the strap around his neck.

"Dad?" he asked the old man. "What hurts?"

"Chest. Feels like. A train. On it."

"Go get the first aid kit," Vic ordered her, his tone composed, but forceful. Charlotte went right away, no longer concerned that the girls, who were now racing behind Alex on their way up the river bank, would be alarmed. All of her worry was saved for Commodore.

"I think he's having a heart attack," Vic said when Alex dropped to his knees beside his grandpa at the same time Charlotte returned with the first aid kit. "There should be some aspirin in there. Give him one and get ready to start CPR if you need to. I'm going to the ranger's station to radio in for a medevac."

"Just…" Commodore tried to say again, but the roar of Vic driving off in the ATV cut him off.

"Don't talk, Com," Alex said, lifting his grandfather's head. "Charlotte, hand me an aspirin. Elsa, go get me that bottle of water we just filled."

Alex checked the older man's pulse as he calmly issued instructions to both her and the girls. "Put the aspirin on his tongue. Give him another sip of water. Grab him a blanket. Find the emergency flare kit, just in case."

Everyone was assigned a task and once they'd completed it, Alex would give them another. Charlotte was about to ask why he needed Audrey to go count how many marshmallows they had left when she heard a sound she didn't think she'd ever hear again. The thwop-thwop-thwop of the rescue chopper.

Wiping away tears of relief, she gathered her daughters to her and huddled with them against the wind as the pilot set the helicopter down. Two paramedics wearing flight suits and helmets jumped out and, carrying narrow yellow stretcher, did a squatting run toward them.

Charlotte couldn't hear what the medics were saying to Commodore and Alex over the turbine engine; however, when they loaded the older man onto the gurney, Elsa pushed past her and ran to Com's side.

"He's my great-grandpa," Elsa yelled out to the paramedic as she snatched Com's weak hand in her smaller one, carefully stroking the stub of his half thumb. "I'm coming with him."

Another chunk crumbled off of Charlotte's heart.

"Sorry, but no family members allowed on the aircraft," the medic replied, and Charlotte bit her lip to keep from pointing out that they weren't truly family anyway. "We're taking him to Shadowview since that's the nearest trauma center, and you can see your great-grandpa there."

"Wait," Elsa shouted, pointing to the oxygen mask. "When he gets that thing off his face, he's gonna want one of these."

Her daughter pulled a toothpick out of her pocket and handed it to the paramedic. More heart crumbling. At this rate, Charlotte would be lucky to get back to San Francisco with half her organ still intact.

She let the wind whip her bangs into her eyes and took each of her daughter's hands in her own, watching as the tail rotor whipped to life again. When the helicopter lifted off, she turned to Alex and saw that he was standing on the other side of Audrey, her tiny palm enveloped in his big grasp.

If Charlotte hadn't been so worried about Commodore, she might've laughed at the fact that she'd spent the morning warning herself about falling for the pretense that she and Alex could share anything more than one night in a tent. Yet here they stood, holding hands with her daughters, looking like the epitome of a caring and concerned family.

Like a perfectly staged scene, Charlotte didn't know what was real and what was just for appearances anymore.

Chapter Ten

The second he'd seen Commodore lying on the ground with Charlotte kneeling next to him, Alex's world had been shaken like never before. Sure, they'd had their share of serious injuries on past camping trips and this wasn't even his first medical evacuation. But none of those other incidents involved *his* grandfather. *His* family.

"He'll be fine," Alex said, more to himself than to reassure Charlotte and the girls. "He's a tough old coot."

"But I wanted to ride in the helicopter with him," Elsa folded her arms across her chest. "What if he gets scared?"

Little Audrey tugged on his hand and pointed to the copse of trees.

"Here comes Grandpa Vic now," Alex said, then

rolled his eyes at his own use of the honorary title. "We'll pack up the campsite and meet Com at the hospital. How does that sound?"

He looked at Charlotte, to see how she would react to his presumptuous offer to take the girls to an emergency room. Her eyes were a mix of blue and purple, as if she hadn't quite made up her mind, and she bit her lip before saying, "I doubt it would be proper for us to go with you guys. It probably should just be family."

"But we *are* his family, Mommy." Elsa stomped her foot, her chubby cheeks turning an angry shade of pink. "Tell her, Grandpa Vic. We're your family, right? Tell her Com would *want* to see his granddaughters at the hospital."

Audrey grabbed his father's hand, her tear-stained face turned up to his. Alex knew there was no way he'd be the one to say *no* to these two little girls and wasn't surprised to see his dad lift up the smaller child. "Why don't we start packing our supplies and loading the ATVs? I'll talk to your mom. Okay?"

Charlotte's daughters scampered to their tent and Vic turned to him. "How bad was he?"

"The paramedic said it was too soon to tell, but Com was still fairly responsive when they arrived." He attempted to shrug his shoulders as if they didn't weigh a ton. "So that should be a good sign."

"Would you prefer the girls not see him until we're sure that he's stable?" Vic asked Charlotte. "We can bring them to the hospital once we know more."

Alex thought that with the way she'd abruptly walked away from him last night, she wouldn't want her children to ever see *any* of them again. His eyes widened when she said, "I think that would be for the best."

He told himself that she was probably just saying as much to be polite. She'd most likely find an excuse to exit stage right the first chance she got. As they packed up their supplies, Alex didn't allow himself to think about his grandfather or Charlotte or anything that would cause his heart to shrink or his stomach to roil in turmoil. They shoved tents inside sleeping bag duffels and threw fishing tackle in with the wet clothes. He could sort everything out later…after the doctors assured him that Com would be all right.

The whole process, including the ride back to the ranger station where they'd left their cars, took less than an hour, but it felt like an eternity. He should have been surprised to see Kylie waiting there for them, but Alex was operating in a trance-like state by this point and wouldn't have been surprised to see half the town there.

"Matt Cooper heard about Commodore from dispatch and then called me," Kylie explained. "I'll take the girls and this stuff home. Charlotte, why don't you drive Vic and Alex to the hospital?"

Although Vic was always cool and calm under pressure, this morning his dad was a bit too calm, as though he was acting on autopilot, as well. It was why Alex had made Charlotte and her daughters ride in the ATV with him.

But with each passing minute, Alex had retreated a little more into the numbness, trying not to worry about his grandfather's health. At this point, it was probably safer for everyone that he not drive an actual car on a real highway with other motorists. But there was no way Charlotte, with her dislike of hospitals—and now him—would want to take them.

"It's fine," he told Charlotte. "You don't have to go if you don't want to."

He held his breath, a small part of him hoping she would leave once and for all right now. The other ninety-nine percent of him desperately prayed that she would come.

"Let's go," she said, grabbing the keys to the silver Jeep. The knot in Alex's throat dissolved and relief flooded into his lungs. She spoke to her daughters briefly, and Alex heard Kylie promising to bring the girls as soon as they made get-well cards and Commodore's doctors said it was okay to visit. There might've even been some bribing involving frozen waffles, but anxiety was pulsing behind his ears.

Alex immediately got in the backseat and tried not to stare at Charlotte's profile as she drove. He forced his ears to listen as Vic called the hospital to see if Com had arrived and to try to get an update, but Alex's eyes kept straying toward Charlotte. When they arrived at Shadowview forty-five minutes later, his father still didn't have any more answers and Alex's nerves were even more numb. Charlotte, who had seemed like the most level-headed one of all of them up until this point, suddenly looked pale and hung back behind Vic as they approached the reception desk inside the emergency room.

An older man with a shiny bald head, a faded tattoo of an anchor on his forearm and wearing a volunteer's smock searched his computer before saying, "It's showing me that Cuthbert Russell has been taken to the Coronary Care Unit."

Charlotte leaned toward Alex and whispered out the side of her mouth. "Cuthbert? No wonder he goes by Commodore."

Her reaction to hearing the odd name struck Alex as funny, and though he knew the timing was completely inappropriate, he snickered. Charlotte's lips began twitching and all the built-up feelings of the past two weeks flooded Alex's emotional dam and he completely lost it.

"You two knock it off," Vic said, trying to sound stern, and that's when Charlotte dissolved into a fit of giggles. It was like laughing during a church service, where the more he tried to stop, the harder he laughed. His body shook and tears filled his eyes and Alex couldn't stop the tide.

"I'll be damned," the volunteer's deep voice announced, and Alex braced himself for a severe chastisement. But the bald man came around the desk and shook Charlotte's hand instead. "You're Charlotte Folsom! From *Fine Tastes* magazine and those online videos."

The man's words were like a frigid rogue wave capsizing Alex's boat and he sobered up immediately. He saw the second Charlotte put the polite beauty-pageant smile into place before saying, "It's a pleasure to meet you."

"I've read all your articles and follow your blog. I even saw that special you did on the Food Channel last year. My missus heard you were up near Sugar Falls doing a camping story. Wait 'til I tell her I got to meet you in person. She'll be so excited! Would you mind giving me an autograph?" The man reached below the desk and pulled out a faded ball cap embroidered with the words Navy Vet No Regret.

"Actually, sir," Charlotte lowered her voice. "We're in quite a hurry to see Mr. Russell, but perhaps I could sign something for you before I leave?"

"Oh, of course." Thankfully, the volunteer didn't point out that they hadn't been in all that much of a hurry when they'd been giggling like schoolgirls about the name Cuthbert. "That'd be great. In fact, I'll walk you to the Coronary Care Unit myself."

His father shot them all a look as though to say, *Can we get moving, here?* And since that came from the normally laid-back Vic Russell, Alex knew everyone's stress level was on high alert.

"You don't have to do that." Charlotte must have sensed Vic's impatience, as well.

"It's no problem," the volunteer gushed, before snapping at a young orderly walking by. "Trang, cover the desk for me."

As he and his father followed Charlotte and her number one fan, Alex tried to put up a wall of indifference, as if being with a recognizable celebrity was something he dealt with on a daily basis. But the foundation under his wall was like the soft mud on the riverbank. It was just a matter of time before the whole thing washed away and left him raw and exposed to the elements.

At least the sound of Commodore's protesting voice as they approached the partitioned room gave Alex a bit of hope and restored that feeling of normalcy.

"I ain't staying the damn night in this place," Commodore shouted loud enough for the patients in the respiratory recovery unit two wings away to hear. Alex and Vic both picked up their pace.

Charlotte was quick enough to dodge the X-ray image flying out of the room, but the starstruck volunteer wasn't so lucky.

"Cease fire, Com," Alex warned before entering the battle zone, doubtful the retractable curtain would protect him in the event his ornery grandfather decided to launch another projectile in anger.

"Took you guys long enough to show up." Commodore looked at Vic, but Alex's dad was busy apologizing to the volunteer, who was now sporting a red mark on his smooth, shiny head. "Alex, tell them I'm fine and that you're taking me home."

"How are you doing, Commodore?" Charlotte was the only one brave enough to venture close to the side of the hospital bed. Even the doctor, who looked like he played linebacker for a professional football team when he wasn't wearing his white lab coat stenciled with the name Dr. Robinson, seemed hesitant to get too close to the patient.

Seeing Charlotte must've soothed the beast somewhat, though, because Com didn't yell when he responded. "They're trying to make me pay for a bunch of fancy tests I don't need. Probably gonna stick me with that helicopter bill, too. But there ain't a dang thing wrong with me."

"Listen, Mr. Russell." Dr. Robinson glanced down at his file, then back up. "May I call you Cuthbert?"

Charlotte's hand flew to her mouth and Alex had to gulp several times to keep the laughter from starting again. But the little machine monitoring Com's pulse beeped out a warning and his grandfather shouted, "The only thing you can call me is a stinkin' taxi."

Vic held up his hands. "Dad, stop it before they have to sedate you." Dr. Robinson looked hopeful at that idea.

"Why don't I stay here with Commodore—" Charlotte nodded toward the nurse's station, which was surrounded by a full audience "—while you two go and talk to the doctor outside?"

Alex could have kissed her at that moment, but Dr. Robinson was quick to usher him out. What would they have done without Charlotte there to help calm the situation down? Well, sedation, obviously, Alex thought as he looked at the unconscious patient in the room next to Com's.

The doctor led them to an empty alcove near the nurse's station. "The EKG results showed Mr. Russell definitely suffered a heart attack. He's stable now, but we're not sure for how long. We've done a chest X-ray, which shows some damage, but I'd like to do an angiogram right away to check for blockage."

"Does he need surgery?" Alex asked.

"Possibly, but we won't know for sure until we get all the tests done. We'd like to start him on some beta blockers and ACE inhibitors as a precaution, however, he has refused medication and threatened to pull out his IV."

"He doesn't like hospitals," Vic offered. "Or doctors."

"Or anybody, really." Alex tried to soften the insult. "Do you have any suggestions on how to talk to combative, cantankerous old men?"

"I was going to ask you the same question," Dr. Robinson responded.

"We'll see what we can do," Vic said, looking no more confident than Alex felt.

Getting the older man to calm down had apparently fallen squarely on Charlotte's shoulders.

"Com, the girls are terribly worried about you and I can't bring them here to visit until after you get the tests done." Guilt rained down upon her as she said the words, but Charlotte had tried every reason she could think of and was now bringing out the big guns. The old man's affection for her daughters. It was wrong on so many levels, namely because, deep down, she knew she was fostering a relationship that she could never maintain. Not if she wanted to avoid seeing Alex again.

The girls would miss the Russell men, probably more than they missed their own father, since Mitchell hadn't been very involved in their care and they'd been so young when he'd gone to prison. But children were resilient and would get over it soon enough.

Oh, God. She sucked in her cheeks before readjusting her headband. Her mother had said the same thing about her when the school nurse had called to find out when her parents would be arriving for Charlotte's emergency appendectomy surgery. Instead of rushing to her side, her father had faxed a release to the ER doctors allowing them to treat his nine-year-old child, and her mother's assistant sent a bouquet of ugly mums with a typed card that said, *Get Well, Carmichael and Lila Folsom.* She'd hated hospitals ever since.

"How long are these tests supposed to take?" Com asked, and she sensed the older man was caving.

"Let me find out." Charlotte stepped into the hall and froze at the bustling activity around her. She didn't blame Commodore a bit for wanting to get out of this place. It was damn scary. The machines were intimidating, the scent of industrial disinfectant and bodily fluids was nauseating and the fear of being left alone to die of some mystery illness was paralyzing. But she wasn't nine anymore, she told her quivering stomach. And she wasn't alone in this huge hospital.

Or was she? Her breath came quicker as she looked around for Alex and Vic, her knees becoming wobbly when she couldn't immediately find them.

"Charlotte?" Alex stepped out of a space adjacent to the nurse's station and she all but collapsed into him. "Is he okay?"

She wiped the dampness from her brow, allowing her eyes to focus on him. "I think so. He wants to know how long the tests will take."

"My dad is going over that with the doctor now. Are *you* okay?"

It took several attempts to push her trembling lips into a smile, but she was finally able to paste one on. "Of course," she said, more as an observation to herself. "I should probably check in and let the girls know what's going on. I had to promise your grandfather that I'd let them come visit once he did the testing."

"It's like negotiating with a terrorist," Alex said. "I don't know why he's being so stubborn."

"Some people don't like hospitals," she said, ignoring the way he tilted his head at her. The question in his eyes. "It's actually a rather common fear."

"Commodore Russell isn't afraid of anything. At least, according to him."

"I think he'd feel better if you or your dad stayed here with him. I know I wouldn't want to be all alone…" Her voice trailed off. It wasn't important what she would want. This wasn't her medical crisis. It wasn't her family. "I'm going to head down to the lobby and call Kylie."

"Wait. Will you stay for a few more minutes while the doctor talks us through everything? I have a feeling Com will be less likely to raise his voice if you're in the room."

"Sure," she said, doubting that Alex was any more clear on her role here than she was. All she knew was that he needed her, or at least, his grandfather did, and that Charlotte couldn't tell him no. Despite the fact that she would much rather be swirling under the rapids of Sugar River than in this place right now—despite the fact that her legs were frozen in place—Charlotte liked being needed. It meant she wasn't alone.

"Come on." He grabbed her hand and gently nudged her out of the hallway.

Vic and the cardiologist that had been in Com's room when they'd first arrived followed her and Alex inside. Commodore's sagging shoulders squared back up the second his eyes spotted the white lab coat and she immediately went to his side and took his hand in her own.

As Dr. Robinson explained the procedure for the angiogram, the old man's gnarled fingers squeezed hers and she found herself squeezing back, trying to reassure him and herself. They couldn't schedule the test until the following morning and wanted to keep Commodore here under observation. His hand was trembling slightly and Charlotte knew a proud man like him wouldn't want his only son and grandson to see his fear. When the cardiologist left, she found herself volunteering to stay through the night.

"No. You gotta go get my honorary great-grand-daughters and bring them in for a visit. I don't want those angels worrying themselves sick about what's wrong. Vic or Alex can stay with me."

Initially, she'd thought the older man had been indulging the girls by allowing them to call him grandpa. But there was no reason for him to keep up the pretense when they weren't here. Now, Charlotte felt all the more guilty for only thinking of her daughters' resiliency.

Would the senior Russell, along with Vic, have just as difficult a time bouncing back when Charlotte and the girls returned to San Francisco? She was kicking herself at thought of causing them unnecessary distress. It was why she and Alex had agreed upon no strings in the first place. This whole one-big-happy-family charade was going too far and now they would all end up getting hurt in the long run.

Part of her wanted to invent an excuse as to why she couldn't bring the girls to see him. But Com's normally robust body looked so fragile in that hospital gown with all those tubes attached to him. Charlotte couldn't weaken his spirit, either—no matter how nauseous her tummy grew at the thought of setting foot in this sterile, cold environment twice in one day.

She couldn't hear Vic's and Alex's lowered voices as they stood huddled in the corner, but it was plain to see that some sort of negotiation was furiously underway. Even Audrey and Elsa had enough manners to know not to whisper in front of people like that. She coughed to get their attention. "So which one of you is staying here and who is coming back to Sugar Falls with me?"

"Dad is staying." Alex shoved his father forward and Vic shot a look at his son as though he was vowing to get retribution for the deal he'd probably just lost. "I have to unpack all the camping supplies and check in at the store."

Some of the tension eased in Charlotte's shoulders. It was almost noon. If she planned it right, she could have him drop her off at Kylie's, then bring the girls to the hospital to visit Com before Alex got done with everything and came back. Maybe she could even rent a car and leave straight from the hospital and keep on driving to San Francisco. She'd ask her friend to ship the rest of their stuff home.

She fished the keys to the Jeep out of her tote bag. "Well then, we better get going if we want to make it back in time for visiting hours."

"I'm starved," Commodore said when she bent to kiss his weathered cheek. "Bring back some of Freckles' fried chicken with you. Or a double bacon cheeseburger from the café."

"No, Dad." Vic rolled his eyes and reiterated the doctor's orders for a low-fat, low-sodium diet, while she followed Alex's cue to leave the room.

"Then sneak something in," Com yelled out, making several nurses and a white-haired lady wearing a purple robe and pushing her IV pole swivel their heads toward them. Great. Not only was Charlotte already dreading coming back, but all the staff would be suspiciously eyeballing her as if she were some sort of rule breaker staging a coup. Alex took her hand as they walked down the hall and she forced herself to put one foot in front of the other.

"Someday," he said when the elevator doors closed, "you can tell me why being in a hospital terrifies you so badly."

Someday. Her trembling belly did a somersault. He said it as if he planned to see her again. And she forced a smile as if she planned to stick around.

Chapter Eleven

Charlotte insisted on driving the Jeep back to the Gregsons', which was just as well because Alex needed to make some phone calls. First, he called Kylie to update her on his grandfather's condition and to pass along Charlotte's message that she would take the girls to visit Commodore this afternoon. Then he spoke with Wilson Masuno, one of the college kids they'd hired for the summer, to let him know they'd need to do some rescheduling for upcoming trips.

By the time he responded to Matt Cooper's text, his stomach was doing an imitation of an angry grizzly bear. He had no idea what had happened to the beautiful breakfast Charlotte cooked this morning before Com's heart attack, but, like him, he was pretty sure she hadn't had anything since dinner last night. "You want to stop and grab a bite to eat at Patrelli's?"

"Where?" she asked, as though he'd interrupted her from her own thoughts.

"The Italian restaurant downtown on Snowflake Boulevard. They're open for lunch and I'm starving."

She brushed her bangs away from her forehead, then darted her eyes his way a couple of times. "Do you think that would be...uh...improper?"

"Charlotte, its lunch. Not a date." He spit out the last word too defensively. "It's not like you need a chaperone."

"I didn't mean it *that* way." Of course she didn't. Because that would imply that she had the slightest bit of romantic feeling toward him. "I was just thinking that with Commodore in the hospital, people might think it's odd that we're...that *you're* not with him."

"Anyone who knows Com will know exactly why I'm not with him. And they'll pity my dad for drawing the short straw. My grandfather's dislike of doctors, government officials and fresh produce is common knowledge around here."

She bit her lip and he could see the gears turning in her mind. Alex was about to tell her not to do him any favors when she said, "I let Audrey and Elsa feed the blueberry pancakes to some squirrels earlier, so I guess I'm pretty hungry."

He tried not to pump his fist in triumph. They were going to have a meal together. In public. Just the two of them. Like a real date. Except she'd made it clear that she had no desire to date him. And she was probably only agreeing out of starvation and sympathy because his grandfather was in the hospital.

Still. He'd take whatever he could get.

She parked the Jeep on Snowflake Boulevard and

sent a text message to Kylie telling her where they were going. Alex held open the wide oak door and the smell of garlic and pizza dough made his mouth water.

It was after the lunch rush and the dim restaurant was nearly empty. One of the six Patrelli kids sat them at a booth near the back and Mrs. Patrelli came out of the kitchen, wiping her hands on her white apron and yelling across the dining room, "How's your grandpa, Alex?"

"News travels fast," Charlotte whispered.

"That's small town life for you," Alex muttered out of the corner of his mouth before standing and allowing the full-figured woman to pull him in for a hug. "He's stable. They're going to keep him overnight and run some tests."

"Those poor nurses are gonna have their hands full," Mrs. Patrelli said, pulling rosary beads out of her apron pocket. "I sure hope they sedate him."

Before Alex could make introductions, the woman turned to Charlotte and pulled her up out of her seat for a hug, as well. "It's an honor to have you in our restaurant, Miss Folsom. I'm Carla Patrelli. I heard you were in town and staying with the Gregsons, and told Kylie that if she didn't bring you by, I'd never serve her another garlic knot."

"It's a pleasure to meet you, Mrs. Patrelli," Charlotte said, giving another award-winning smile. "I've heard wonderful things about your menu."

"Well, I try to stick with most of the traditional Patrelli family dishes, but I tried that eggplant piccata recipe from your vegetarian series last fall and even my meat-eating customers went wild for it. Hey, Jo-Jo," Mrs. Patrelli called out to her teenage son who was bussing some tables. "Come take a picture of me with Miss Folsom. My sister-in-law over in Chicago is gonna die when I tell her I met you."

Alex shook his head and thought about going into the kitchen and making his own lunch. As far as fan recognition went, this was almost as bad as the bald volunteer at the hospital who wanted Charlotte to sign his hat. So much for alone time with her.

It took almost ten minutes for them to order since Mrs. Patrelli explained all the specialty dishes to Charlotte, despite the fact that descriptions were written on the menu next to each item.

"Do you ever get tired of this?" Alex asked when the restaurant owner bustled off to get them a bottle of red wine on the house.

"Of what?"

"This." Alex made a circular motion with his hand. "The celebrity treatment. People making a big deal about you everywhere you go."

"Would it bother *you?*" Charlotte turned the question back on him and he had to think about it.

She took one of the garlic knots out of the basket and set it on his bread plate. She was always doing stuff like that. Serving others before she served herself.

"Of course," he replied, then tried to soften his tone. "I'm a private person. I don't like everyone knowing my business."

"And yet you live in Sugar Falls."

"Exactly," he said, then noticed her *ah-ha* look, as if she'd just trapped him into admitting something. "Wait. Why do you look so smug?"

"Since I've met you, we've run into way more people that know *you* than know me. I'd say *you're* the celebrity, Alex."

"That's ridiculous," he said, then thanked twelve-year-old Kayla, the youngest Patrelli, for bringing their Caesar salads.

"Do you know what color our wilderness camp shirts are going to be this year, Mr. Russell?" Kayla asked. "Last year all the girls had to wear that horrible grayish-blue color the boys picked, so this year I think we should do fuchsia."

"We'll vote on it, Kayla," Alex said. "You should start canvassing the neighborhood and get the campaign started."

Charlotte smirked again as the girl left. "See what I mean?"

"No." Alex shook his head before lifting a forkful of salad. "You'll have to explain it."

"Scooter, the old cowboy who rode on horseback with the rescue team said not to worry about leaving your fishing gear behind because he knows how you like your tackle box organized. The fish and game warden who drove the ATV when we first got rescued asked if his son was going to be on your Pop Warner team this year. Garcia, the paramedic, made a joke about your grandfather's attitude toward oxygen masks. Drew Gregson reminded you of how many cookies you lost to him two weeks ago at poker night. Chief Cooper knows where you leave the spare set of keys to your Jeep. Freckles doesn't have to write down how you like your eggs—scrambled with cheese." Charlotte delicately picked up her own fork and asked, "Should I go on?"

"So the people around here know me." Alex moved

his salad plate to the side to make room for the gnoc-
chi in alfredo sauce he'd ordered. At this rate, he was
going to have to unbutton his waistband before lunch
was over. "It's a small town."

"Well, my readers are *my* small town. Did you know
it's actually relatively easy to go unnoticed in a big city,
to just become one of millions and to lose yourself?
Growing up, it was even easier for me to be overlooked
by my own parents or the teachers who left campus on
the weekends and holidays. Do you have any idea how
lonely that can be?"

Alex used his napkin to wipe his mouth, his appe-
tite replaced with a heavy anchor of shame for all the
assumptions he'd made about Charlotte Folsom.

Her cheeks were flushed, her eyes were a stormy
shade of violet and her voice was passionate. "I had
to create my own community, my own place where
I belonged. Sometimes, it feels good to have people
know me—or, at least, think they know me—because
it signifies that I'm not alone. It's not like I'm out there
seeking rock-star fame and movie stardom. I cook food
and I give lifestyle tips and I decorate spaces. I create environments that give people comfort and enrich
their lives. So when a stranger stops me on the street
to appreciate my work, it lets me know that I matter
to someone. Just like you and your family's business
matter to this small town."

Alex took a sip of the wine he hadn't ordered, and
studied her. His heart urged him to pull her into his
arms and tell her exactly how much she mattered to
him, but his brain knew that wouldn't solve anything.

What could someone like him offer her? Just because her world made more sense to him now, didn't mean he belonged in it. Or that he ever could.

Charlotte sensed that there was a lot more Alex wanted to say, but her senses when it came to men had been wrong before. Thankfully, before the conversation could turn any more personal than it already had, Kylie maneuvered her double stroller through the door with Elsa and Audrey following behind. She hadn't told Alex that when she'd texted her friend, Charlotte had also hinted to her that the girls might like to stop by for some pizza. Safety in numbers and all that.

"How's Grandpa Commodore, Mommy?" Elsa ran straight to her, making the crease in Charlotte's forehead feel as though it was going to be embedded there permanently.

She wanted to respond that he wasn't Elsa's grandfather, but how could she break the little girl's heart like that? Especially when her own heart was breaking enough for all of them. Besides, she saw the way Elsa was twisting a coloring book in her tiny hands along with the concern etched all over Audrey's wide-eyed face. She also saw that her youngest child's legs were frozen together and her arms were still at her sides.

"What's Audrey pretending to be?" Charlotte asked Kylie, who was distracted with strapping one of her twins into a wooden high chair at the table next to them.

"A toothpick," Elsa said before lowering her voice to a whisper. "I wanted her to be an oxygen mask, but she thought Grandpa Com didn't look as happy with that thing on his mouth."

Charlotte knelt down on the black-and-white checkered tile floor. "Come here," she said, pulling both of her daughters in for a hug. "Gran… Commodore is doing much, much better. The doctor thinks that he can maybe come home tomorrow."

"Is that true?" Elsa looked at Alex, and something clogged in Charlotte's throat. Did her own daughter doubt her? "Mommy always tells us that people are going to get better, but then they never come back."

Charlotte's head jerked back as if she'd been slapped. "What do you mean?"

"You said Daddy made a bad mistake and was going to get re-bilitated. But we haven't seen him in a long time. And your mom, Lila—" Charlotte cringed at the little girl's use of her own grandmother's first name "—left to get that operation on her face and she never camed back, either."

Audrey, displaying a rare lack of commitment to her inanimate object role, swiped at her eyes, her little dimpled chin tucked into her chest. Charlotte's throat constricted even more and she had to wipe the dampness of her palms onto the backs of her daughters' matching floral smocked rompers. Perhaps she did have a habit of softening the blows and telling the girls what she thought they should hear rather than the truth. Yes, their father was in prison and would likely never be released. And, no her mother didn't possess an ounce of grandmotherly warmth and was more comfortable in her plastic surgeon's recovery room than at a child's birthday party.

Charlotte opened and closed her mouth, trying to find the words to allay the girls' skepticism. Instead, she felt Alex's knee brush alongside her hip as he knelt beside her.

"Huddle up, ladies," he said, pulling them in close. "Your mom is right. Grandpa Commodore is going to be just fine. In fact, he was asking if you all would like to come visit him at the hospital today. The doctor needs to do a big test where they take a special kind of X-ray picture of his heart and Com was real nervous." Alex nodded toward Elsa's coloring book. "Maybe you could draw him a picture or write him a little note telling him to be brave?"

Both of the girls nodded before running and asking Kylie for their crayons and setting themselves up at the bigger table where the twin babies were playing with plastic straws.

And just like that, it was Alex Russell to the rescue again. Handsome, strong, capable of climbing mountains Alex Russell. How would she ever get over him?

Deep down, she knew she wouldn't.

She massaged her pounding temples. Charlotte had thought she'd been doing an okay job as a single mother until she'd visited Sugar Falls and experienced the concept that it really does take a village to raise a child. Unfortunately, this wasn't her village. And the sooner she got back to San Francisco, the sooner they could all put this cozy little Idaho town behind them.

Kylie ordered pizza for the girls and Alex excused himself to go check on the store. "Do you want me drop you off on my way?" he asked Charlotte.

"Actually, I'll stay here with Kylie and then I'll drive the girls down to Shadowview to see Commodore." Calling the place by its name made the hospital seem less impersonal. Less imposing. See? She was already getting better at facing her insecurities all on her own.

Audrey stood up on her chair to give Alex a hug

goodbye and Elsa, impatient and unwilling to be out-done, sandwiched her sister as she wrapped her chubby, tan arms around Alex's neck. Charlotte didn't have the heart to tell any of them that this was actually goodbye for good. For real this time.

She was too busy curving her feet around the legs of the chair, locking herself into place to keep from following her daughters' lead and jumping up into his arms right along with them.

Kylie had given her this same strange look all through lunch at Patrelli's and, as Charlotte packed their suitcases an hour later, the questioning stare only grew more intense. The twins were down for their nap and Audrey and Elsa were busy at the dining room table coloring pictures for Commodore. Which meant Charlotte's friend finally had her cornered in the guest room.

Kylie tucked her thumbs under her armpits and flapped her elbows up and down while making farm animal sounds.

"I'm not being a chicken," Charlotte defended her-self.

"Are you even going to say goodbye to Alex?" Kylie asked.

"I said bye at the restaurant."

"You know what I mean."

"I'm not so good at that kind of thing. You know how my parents are. The Folsoms aren't big on emo-tional displays."

"Charlotte, you are not your parents." Kylie pointed toward out the bedroom door. "Hell, just look at what an amazing mom you are to those two little girls out there. Your entire life is dedicated to them and making sure they're always taken care of and never alone."

"That's why I'm leaving now. Before they get too attached to this perfect little town and that damn hunky woodsman and develop their own separation anxiety issues."

"Leaving?" Kylie moved her hands down to her hips. "I call it sneaking."

"This isn't sneaking. It's the middle of the afternoon. And we're going to stop by the hosp…by Shadowview our way to the airport and say goodbye to Commodore and Vic. Plus, I have an article to write and Neal wants it done before the magazine's annual Black and White Gala, which is next weekend. Some of the biggest names in publishing are going to be there, along with their marketing directors, and he thinks I have a shot at pitching a concept for a series to one of the major cable networks."

"That doesn't explain why you're cutting out on Alex, and you know it."

The words stung Charlotte because that's exactly what she was doing. "Maybe it's self-preservation then. It's not like Alex is begging me to stay."

"I'm not even going to get started on Alex's abandonment issues," Kylie said, leaning against the doorjamb. Her friend didn't have to bring up Mariah Judge's name to remind Charlotte of another woman who'd walked out of the man's life.

"This is different. I don't owe him anything. No strings attached, remember?"

"I get that, but did it occur to you that he's doing this self-preservation thing, as well?"

Kylie's question echoed in Charlotte's mind as she

drove a rental car to the hospital. Hospital. Hospital. Hospital. There was no getting around where they were. She held each of her daughters' hands in her own as they crossed the parking lot. But her nerves weren't as jumpy this time as she entered the building. She had to be strong for her girls.

Although, judging by the way Audrey was skipping down the linoleum-floored halls and Elsa was waving at every nurse, orderly and patient they passed, telling anyone who would listen that they were going to visit her great-grandpa, Charlotte's children weren't at all nervous about their intimidating surroundings.

They only turned down the wrong hallway once—because all those nurses' stations looked the same to Charlotte—and when they finally arrived in the coronary care unit, Audrey ran ahead to room 308. Several nurses sighed as Vic met them in the doorway and pulled the smaller girl up onto his hip and let her bury her face in his neck. A patient in a wheelchair told the young orderly pushing him that he loved Vic in the Wolverine movies.

"Honey, don't climb up there." Charlotte lunged into the room after Elsa, who was already on the foot of Commodore's bed.

"She's fine," the older man said, scooting his stocky body over to make room for the six-year-old. The machine next to him beeped and Charlotte held her breath, worried that the exertion and excitement was going to send him into cardiac arrest.

She didn't exhale until it became clear that no monitors or alarms were going off. "Just be careful of those tubes," Charlotte said.

Com showed off his IV and the little red light blinking on his finger and the girls used the magnets on the white board to display the get well cards they'd drawn. Charlotte prayed the staff wouldn't notice that one picture was of Prince String Bean eating a brown apple (Elsa explained the fruit was supposed to be from a can, but it looked like more like a small rodent) and the other was of an elk head mounted to a wall with a toothpick in its mouth. The gray smear above the illustrated toothpick gave the impression that the elk was smoking a cigarette.

She had to remind her daughters several times not to touch anything before Vic finally said, "Why don't I take the girls down to the vending machine to get them a snack?"

"Get me some Pop-Tarts," Commodore yelled to his son as Charlotte watched several nurses happily volunteer to escort Alex's hunky father to the cafeteria.

"Us Russell men are cursed with these blasted good looks." Commodore shook his head in disgust and Charlotte had to bite back her laughter. Other than similar coloring, Vic and Alex most assuredly did not take after the elderly Russell in the looks department. "Women can never leave us alone."

Charlotte saw the opening and adjusted her headband before asking, "Then why was Alex's mom able to leave so easily?"

The heart-rate monitor beside Commodore betrayed his attempt to nonchalantly wave his hand. "That gal wouldn't have known a good thing if it'd bit her in her stuck-up city keister."

"You didn't like her?" Charlotte asked.

He sighed. "I saw through all her spiritual growth phony baloney a mile away. But she did give me my grandson and I'll be forever grateful for that. Probably one of the few selfless things that woman ever did."

"Do you think it still affects Alex? Like in his personal life?"

"I don't see why it would," Commodore huffed. "His Granola was all the mom he needed, up until she passed, rest her good soul. After that, his dad and I raised him right and he has plenty of friends. Could you imagine if the boy had grown up in New York with his mom? He'd have been miserable in the big city, going to snobby private schools and being forced to go to all those fancy society balls and what not."

She studied the older man as she thought of the upcoming black tie event she was attending. No, she couldn't imagine Alex fitting into that lifestyle. *Her* lifestyle. Leaving him was really for the best. For all of them.

"So, the girls and I are heading to the airport after this. But we'll keep in touch and I'll have them call you after your procedure tomorrow. Maybe we can come out to visit during the Christmas break." Charlotte hoped Com couldn't detect the false promise in her voice.

He sniffed and the toothpick Elsa had slipped him quivered ever so slightly. "I was hoping you wouldn't take off so soon."

She didn't miss the implication that she would've left eventually. "Well, I have this article to finish and a bunch of work back home that needs my attention. And you guys are going to be so busy the rest of summer with all the business my magazine will be sending your way…"

"Does he know you're leaving?" His steely green gaze left Charlotte with no doubt of who "he" was.

She looked at her small gold watch, the one her father's assistant had sent her the day after her college graduation. She'd told herself that the gift was an extension of her parents' love but its coldness was now weighing her wrist down. She slid the dainty timepiece off and put it in her tote bag. She'd created her own love, her own family, and it was time to get back to the life she'd made for her daughters.

"I'll take that as a no," Com said.

"I'm not sneaking away," Charlotte defended herself for the second time today. "Alex will be relieved that I've gone back to San Francisco."

"Will he?"

"It's like you said. He belongs here in Sugar Falls." Her throat constricted as she forced out the next words. "He doesn't need me."

"It don't matter what he thinks he needs. What do *you* need?"

Charlotte needed to feel needed. How pathetic was that? She wanted to take care of Alex, to make a home for him. But unless he said otherwise, he was fine without her.

"I need you to rest and get better," she said before leaning in and giving the man a kiss on his rough, paper thin cheek. Then, she did the only thing she could. She took care of her own heart and she left.

"So, just like that?" Alex snapped his fingers. "She said goodbye?"

He and Vic were sitting in the family lounge, waiting for Commodore to wake up from his nap following the angiogram. The cardiologist had said his grandfather wouldn't need bypass surgery, but prescribed several new medications and a healthier diet—which would be enough to give the old man another heart attack. Com hated change.

And Alex was finding that he was a lot like his grandfather in that regard.

"She had to get back to work, son." Vic shrugged his shoulders. The complacent gesture infuriated Alex.

"Did you at least try and talk her into staying?"

"When she told me she was leaving, we were in the hallway outside by the vending machines and I couldn't say anything in front of the girls. Even if I could, it wasn't my place."

"Yeah, just like it wasn't your place to talk my mom into staying, either."

Vic looked up to the ceiling, the only telltale sign that Alex had flustered his dad. "Who says I didn't try and talk her into it?"

"Actually, Dad, nobody actually said you didn't, because we've never talked about it. Not once. And it's not like I can ask Mariah Judge why she gave me up so easily before hightailing it back to New York before I was even a month old. She's dead."

"What did you want me to say?" Vic asked. "That she never wanted to be a mother? A wife? You never wanted to talk about it and I thought she'd made her decision pretty clear. She wasn't like Charlotte, you know."

Alex flinched at the comparison. "What do you mean?"

"There was nothing nurturing about Mariah. I don't mean that in a bad way, but mothering doesn't come naturally to every woman. When I met her, she was almost forty and I was this young college student from some mountain town in the middle of nowhere. Her life had been established and I'd barely had mine mapped out. She was beautiful and smart and hardworking, but she knew exactly what she wanted and you and I weren't in the equation."

"Did you try to convince her otherwise?"

"As a matter of fact, I did. I moved to New York City for all of a month and did a pretty good job of pretending that I didn't hate it there. But there was no convincing Mariah. She sent me back with the promise that she'd return to Boise for her due date."

"I'm surprised you got her to agree to leave New York again."

"Well, she was writing speeches for a certain United States senator with a scandalous record and didn't want the press to catch wind of her pregnancy and make any assumptions. But, after your grandfather showed her his birthing quilt, Mariah refused to be out of a five-mile range from the nearest modern hospital. So Boise it was." Vic put his arm around Alex, squeezing his son's shoulder. "Giving you to me didn't make her a bad person. She couldn't help who she was or how she felt. In fact, I think she must have loved you an awful lot to recognize that in herself and to completely entrust you to my care."

The tightness in Alex's chest loosened. "Did she at least attempt to stay in touch at all?"

He tried to tell himself that it didn't matter. That he'd been better off being raised by his family in Sugar Falls.

Vic looked up to the ceiling again. "She called

once, right before her book came out, to give me the heads-up and to explain why she never published anything specific about me. Or you."

Alex snorted. "Probably because she didn't want to jeopardize her career if people found out she'd abandoned her kid."

But saying the words out loud again didn't have the same sting as they'd had when he was a kid with the thought passing through his mind.

"Actually, it was because she wanted to protect our privacy. She knew that I wasn't comfortable with all that limelight and she wanted to be respectful of that. I know it must have felt that way. And I've always tried to make up for what she did. But from where I sat, I never saw her leaving you with me as an abandonment." Vic pulled Alex in closer. "I saw it as a gift."

"Excuse me," a woman wearing surgical scrubs said, as she exited the recovery room, the blasting sound of Commodore yelling about his catheter coming from behind her. "You can come back and see Cuthbert now. If you really want to."

The nurse's tone indicated that she wouldn't blame Vic and Alex if they pretended not to hear her or his grandfather's bellowing and snuck away.

"Speaking of gifts," Alex said, trying to lighten the mood. "Maybe we'll wait until after he uses the restroom."

The woman smiled, mostly at Vic, then retreated back into the recovery room.

His dad stood up and stretched. "Mariah set up a trust for you, you know."

Alex did a double take. "Nobody's ever mentioned anything about it before."

"Well, like you said, we never really talked about your mother. I tried to broach the subject once when you turned eighteen, but I always got the impression that you didn't want us ever bringing her up. Mariah was a big believer that people didn't truly find themselves until they were out of their twenties, so it's set up so that you can't access it until you're thirty-five."

"I'll be thirty-five in a year and a half, Dad." He stood up. "When were you going to mention it?

Vic shrugged. "I was waiting for you to ask me about her."

"Not that I want her money, but just out of curiosity, how much are we talking about?"

Vic named a figure and Alex had to sit down again. His dad laughed. "I guess her book is still pretty popular today."

Alex thought about the irony of Charlotte reading *Our Natural Souls*, which she credited with the idea of inspiring her rafting trip. The rafting trip that Alex's family needed to help promote business so they could make up the lost revenue from last year and pay off Com's outstanding tax debt.

The rafting trip that had brought them together for the first time…

But Alex's trust fund would easily pay off that debt several times, with plenty left over to buy a mansion in the heart of San Francisco. If that's where he wanted to live. With Charlotte.

"Do you ever think about what your life would've been like if you would've moved to New York City?" he asked his dad.

"Nope. I don't have to." His dad put his arm around

him again. "Because I went there and found out for myself. And I wasn't even in love."

"Who says I'm in love?"

"Why does everyone think I'm just a pretty face?" Vic shook his head. "Son, I may have only been a kid myself when you were born, but from the second you were in my arms, I've known when you're hungry, when you're tired, when you're trying to hide your feelings.

"Do you remember when you locked yourself in the bottom half of the china cabinet so you wouldn't have to go to Granola's funeral? How hard you were crying, and you didn't want anyone to see? I know when you're scared and when you're annoyed because you didn't want me to invite Chuck Marconi on that mountain bike trip with us. But you never would have confronted him for being a bully if I hadn't. I know when you're too proud to ask for help and insist on going on the river even when a thunderstorm is coming.

"I know the difference between you liking some of the kids on your little league team and you letting yourself get close to a couple of charming little girls with big, inquisitive brown eyes and a lack of a strong male role model. And I sure as hell know when you've fallen for their mother."

The pang of longing in Alex's chest was as unexpected as it was intense, nearly robbing him of breath. He needed to see Charlotte. Just one more time. Just to be sure.

"By any chance would you know what I'd need to do to get her back?"

Chapter Twelve

It turned out that his father's idea for getting Charlotte back involved questioning half the town of Sugar Falls for advice. And everyone at the Cowgirl Up Café had their own ridiculous suggestions.

Kylie had tried to talk Alex into buying a tuxedo before coming to San Francisco, but he wasn't ready to commit to something so expensive and formal. He wasn't even sure if he was willing to commit to moving to the city…or if that's what Charlotte would want. Hell, it'd taken him an entire week to work up the nerve just to fly out here and talk to the woman.

But as he stood outside the Merchants Exchange Building in the Financial District, watching the limos drive up and the camera flashes illuminate the people on the red carpet, he told himself that he would find out if they had a future together. One way or another.

Pasting a bored expression on his face, he slipped past a throng of photographers and ducked behind one of the columns as he made his way through the outer doors. There was a crush of people just inside the entryway and he saw the security guard standing beside the elevator bank with a clipboard, probably checking names on his list. Alex's gut dropped, realizing he might not have thought this out thoroughly. When Kylie and Freckles had come up with this stupid plan—and Commodore had challenged his manhood by betting him five bucks that he wouldn't go through with it— it had never occurred to Alex that he might not get the chance to see Charlotte. To prove to her that he could fit into her world.

But as the crowd grew larger and his lungs seemed to grow smaller inside his rented tux, Alex wondered if he could actually pull this off. Infiltrating a formal, invitation-only gala in the heart of a major metropolis wasn't the same as swinging by the Friday night fish fry at the Sugar Falls Elks Lodge. And convincing Charlotte that they belonged together wasn't the same as convincing Com that instant mashed potatoes didn't count as a vegetable. Actually, the former might be easier. Still, the doubt reverberating inside him was as uncomfortable as this ridiculous outfit. He looked at his reflection in a gilt framed mirror suspended on the wall in the lobby and checked out his footwear. At least Alex had had the foresight to wear his own boots.

He was about to hide out in the men's room and give himself a better pep talk when he saw Classy Neal step into the building. Charlotte's editor had sent Commodore a large floral arrangement after his release from the hospital, and while his grandfather had complained about the fussiness of the flowers and the wasted expense, Com had appreciated the editor's thoughtful gift more than the fresh fruit basket Mrs. Cromartie of Auntie's Antiques had delivered.

Neal would surely remember Alex and pull some strings to get him in the ballroom doors. Otherwise, he'd be forced to sit out in the lobby, waiting for Charlotte. Or worse, drive back home with his tail between his legs.

Several people were surrounding the editor of *Fine Tastes* and it took quite a few attempts for Alex to get the man's attention. When he finally did, Alex had to reintroduce himself since the guy clearly didn't remember him.

"I was Charlotte Folsom's river guide out in Sugar Falls."

"You're kidding," Neal said, studying him before turning to a young guy Alex recognized as the production assistant who'd come into the store to check out the tent colors. "If our readers thought the rugged mountain man was sexy in all that flannel, wait until they see him in Hugo Boss."

Alex steeled his jaw and clenched his fists. He wasn't here for a commentary on his appearance. Although, the reassurance was a slight balm to his already fragile ego. "I'm looking for Charlotte but I don't think she remembered to put me on the guest list."

"Nonsense." Neal did that finger steepling thing again. "Charlotte never forgets a list. But you're here now and the opportunity for a good before and after picture is too big to pass up."

The man pointed at his assistant. "Finn, go get one

of the cameramen and meet us upstairs in the ballroom."

Alex would've agreed to a cover shoot if it meant he could talk to Charlotte. Biting his tongue, he followed Neal into the elevator and rode with him and twenty or so other party goers up to the Julia Morgan Ballroom, pretending the ascent was the only thing making him sick to his stomach.

When Alex stepped out of the filigreed doors, he felt as though he was crossing into an alternate dimension. The glitz and the glamour were heavy on his eyes and he squinted to see past all the beautiful people in their beautiful clothes standing around the beautiful tables centered amidst the stunningly beautiful architecture. Luckily, he was able to ditch Neal, who'd stopped to talk to a herd of reporters standing in a roped-off area.

It was all too much for his hyped-up senses to take in. The ballroom was too warm, the orchestra was too loud and the passing wait staff were too quick. Alex thought about going to the bar to order a drink so he could calm down long enough to acclimate himself to his surroundings. Then he wondered if having a domestic beer would make him appear even more out of place. Man, he wanted to get the hell out of here. But he wanted to see Charlotte more.

Taking a deep breath, he told himself that if he could survive this, he could survive anything.

Alex put one foot in front of the other as if he were wearing hiking boots and starting a twelve-mile uphill trail, and made his way deeper into the crowd. It wasn't until he was halfway across the room that he saw her.

Charlotte.

His legs froze and his pulse skyrocketed and every

word of the speech he'd rehearsed on the ten hour drive out here floated up to the ornate gilded ceiling. She was even more beautiful than he'd remembered. Her dress was subtle, but unique. Black and satiny smooth, it had no sequins, no bows and not an ounce of excessive fabric. In fact, when she pivoted to speak with someone behind her, Alex's breath caught at the bare skin exposed by the deep plunging back.

He'd touched that skin, felt those muscles move as she'd risen above him, and his fingers itched to experience it one more time. Again he thought about making his way to the bar, just to have a drink to keep his hands occupied so he could string together a sentence and talk to her. But before he could decide, Charlotte turned back around and her violet-blue eyes landed on him.

She'd been counting down the minutes until the cocktail hour was over so she could excuse herself and leave the gala. She'd helped plan the event, along with Neal and the creative director for *Fine Tastes*, and she'd normally be right at home in her role as hostess if she wasn't so emotionally drained. For the first time in her life, she cursed her organizational party-planning skills because there was nothing left for her to do but put on a happy face while standing around with various acquaintances, answering questions about her wilderness adventure, her hands nervously toying with the stem of her champagne flute. In fact, she wished she had something more important to do, a last-minute centerpiece crisis or an appetizer catastrophe to see to. Anything that would keep her mind from thinking about how she'd much rather be in the Idaho wilderness than in the middle of a San Francisco landmark.

A cramp formed between her left check and jaw from her forced smile, and her professionally applied makeup was stiff under her swollen eyes—the ones that had spent the previous night crying after Elsa asked if she could read a bedtime story over FaceTime to her grandpas, and Audrey refused to sleep in anything but a makeshift tent in the living room. Charlotte had just told Debra Braxton with the Food Network that she would love to fly into New York to meet with their producers when she turned around and saw the subject of her tears. She blinked several times before downing the bubbly contents of her glass.

Alex Russell in a tuxedo was indeed a sight to behold. She remembered one of her nannies taking her to the lion house once at the San Francisco Zoo. Her seven-year-old heart had broken for the wild and noble animals pacing around their caged habitat, but not as much as her thirty-year-old heart was breaking now. Like those majestic lions, there was something about Alex Russell that couldn't be tamed. That *shouldn't* be tamed.

Her body heated up just by looking at him. What was he doing here?

As he walked toward her, her eyes refused to look away, afraid to find out that she was only seeing what she wanted to see. By the time he was inches away, her knees trembled, her mouth had grown dry and her arms ached to reach out and prove that it was truly him standing before her.

"Hi," he said, as if they'd happened to sit down next to each other at the counter of the Cowgirl Up Café.

"Hi." She tipped the crystal flute up to her lips again, only to realize that she'd finished her champagne already.

"Hi," he said again, before looking around at the crowded ballroom, doubt filling his normally confident green eyes. Suddenly, Charlotte didn't feel like the one in need of rescue this time.

"How's your grandfather?" she asked.

"Ornery," he nodded. "But better."

"Kylie said they released him from the hospital the day after we left." Actually, her friend had used the term "snuck away" but Charlotte wasn't going get into semantics when she was attempting to put him at ease. She waited for him to accuse her of not saying goodbye. But he just stood there, rocking back and forth on his black ostrich cowboy boots. And, while she was relieved to see that, despite the tux, he'd retained a small piece of himself, she couldn't stand his silence. "I had no idea you were coming to San Francisco."

"Neither did I until a few days ago."

"I wish Neal would've told me he sent you an invitation. I would've made sure your name was on the guest list."

Alex glanced over his shoulder at the upstairs security guard standing by the elevators. "Neal didn't invite me. Kylie did."

"Kylie's here?" Charlotte looked behind him for her friend.

"No. She told me I should come. She made me rent this stupid tux and my dad booked me a room at the Omni and Freckles asked me to bring her back some sourdough bread and Com told me to give you this."

Alex was quicker than a pouncing lion when he grabbed Charlotte around the waist and pulled her to him. His mouth claimed hers right there in the center of the Julia Morgan Ballroom in downtown San Francisco and it was just as spectacular as it had been on that mountain in Sugar Falls. Her lips eagerly opened up to him and she decided she liked kissing him hello much better than kissing him goodbye.

When he eventually drew back, his hands still toyed with the low opening on the back of her dress, his fingers splaying possessively across her skin.

He said nothing, and yet, he'd said everything. He still hadn't said what he was doing here, and as much as she wanted to tell herself not to expect anything, every piece of her already crumbled heart prayed that he'd really come all this way just to see her.

"So, how long will you be staying?"

"For as long as it takes you to realize that we belong together."

"You and me?" Her chest expanded with hope and her smile was no longer forced.

But before he could answer, they heard the band leader introduce Neal. Charlotte, not wanting to make a scene during the editor's speech and not willing to let the opportunity to hear Alex express his feelings pass her by, grabbed his hand and pulled him toward the coat check room, where the wraps and coats could muffle their long overdue conversation.

When she turned to face him, he still looked like a caged lion and her need to soothe him warred with her need to make sure she wouldn't be let down again. "Like we belong together as something more than an occasional hook up?"

He cringed at her reminder of what he'd told her the night he'd kissed her in the forest and she knew her words found their mark. "I never should have said that, but I was too afraid to hope for more."

"So if we were together, it wouldn't just be a hook-up?"

"No way. And it'd be a helluva lot more often than occasionally, if I had my way," Alex said before pulling her for another kiss.

"What about Elsa and Audrey?" she asked when she finally came up for a breath.

"I'd want to see them a lot more than occasionally, as well. I know I may seem like the quintessential bachelor, living out in the woods with my dad and grandpa, but that's only because I've held on to my mother's abandonment as a shield against getting too close to another woman. I've always wanted kids. I just needed to the find the right person to have a family with." He kept his arms around her as he studied her face. "Growing up without a mom, I knew that when I decided to become a parent myself, I'd take it as seriously as my own father did. It's why I was so hesitant to get involved with someone unless I knew she was the real deal."

"And how do you know if I'm the real deal?" After the naïve assumptions she'd made about her first husband, she needed Alex to lay everything out for her. She wanted to know his genuine feelings.

"Because I don't need a fancy lifestyle expert to tell me what's missing in my life. The day you and the girls left was the realest heartache I've ever felt."

"I make you feel real?"

"Lord, woman, you ask a lot of questions. Is there a rule book I'm supposed to be following for the best way to win you and your daughters over?"

The champagne she'd gulped down minutes ago suddenly floated to life inside her, making her all bubbly and tingly. "You already won me over. Way before you even met the girls, who have been moping around the house missing you and Vic and Commodore."

She felt the tension leave his shoulders as his lips turned up at the corners. "Good. Now I just need to convince you that I'm not going anywhere, even if it means moving here and supporting you in your career."

Charlotte lifted a hand to her throat as if she could help herself swallow her excitement and confusion. "You want to move here?"

"Yes."

"To the city?" she clarified.

"If that's where you are, then that's where I'm going to be."

"Why?"

"Because I love you, dammit. Why else would someone like me be willing to give up the only life I've known to follow you here?"

Her heart gave a little dance and her toes tingled inside her high heels. "You love me?"

He cupped her cheek and touched the corner of his mouth to her lips. "I love you more than I would've ever thought possible. But if you still want no strings attached, tell me now before Commodore loads up the Jeep with all my belongings and drives it out here to visit his dumplings."

"Oh, those stupid strings. That's been the first rule I've ever wanted to break." She ran her hands through his styled brown hair, hating the gel that was holding it into place. "I love you, Alex Russell. I love who you are and where you live. I could never ask you to uproot your entire life and live somewhere you hate."

"I wouldn't hate it as long as I was with you. It took you leaving for me to realize that my home is wherever you and the girls are. And your job is here. What about the home you made?"

"My magazine is here, Alex, but my job can be anywhere I want it to be. I can write and cook and take pictures from anywhere—even over a campfire by the Sugar River."

"Are you serious? You'd leave all this?" He pointed out of the dim coat room toward the crowded ballroom filled with people she barely knew.

"This was all I'd ever known until I came to Sugar Falls. But then I fell in love with you and with the town and I had to tell myself not to wish for a life I couldn't have. My biggest concern has always been providing my daughters with a warm and loving home. That home can be anywhere as long as it's full of love. I want their childhoods to be happy and consistent and filled with lots of family and friends."

"Well, I can certainly provide the family and friends back in Sugar Falls, if you'd be willing to live there."

"With you?"

"Of course with me!" he said.

Thirty minutes ago, the thought of never seeing Alex Russell again had been nothing but an empty longing in the pit of her stomach. And now they were talking about moving in together.

"Well there *is* a certain retro kitchen in a cabin in

the mountains that I've been dying to update and write about…" She looked up at him expectantly.

"Nope." He chuckled before kissing her again. "No way are we living with my dad and Com."

Epilogue

Two months later, Alex was holding firm to his promise about not living with his family and had even offered Kylie's brother, Kane Chatterson, a bonus if he finished building his and Charlotte's house—which was actually only a few hundred feet away from the cabin on Russell property—before Thanksgiving. Luckily, the condo Kylie had owned before she and Drew got married was available, and Charlotte had been renting it for the summer.

Charlotte was in her element, designing the house and planning their fall nuptials, posting pictures of both on her blog. After sneaking into the Black and White Gala and witnessing firsthand the types of parties she was capable of throwing, Alex had been a bit nervous about seeing eye-to-eye with his bride on their wedding details. But he'd been humbled when he'd seen

Charlotte's ideas for a simple ceremony beneath the twin birch trees behind his family's home and a reception in the rustic old barn on their neighbor's property.

In fact, yesterday, the Food Network called to offer her a three-part series on do-it-yourself wedding menus and Alex decided she needed a break from the tiny condo kitchen to properly celebrate.

After picking his three favorite ladies up this morning, Alex had hoped for a low key breakfast at the Cowgirl Up Café before the girls' soccer game in town. But when he held open the door for Charlotte, Elsa, and Audrey, he wasn't surprised to find his dad and Commodore sitting at the bigger booth waiting for them.

When they saw their grandpas, the girls squealed as if they hadn't just seen them yesterday when Vic and Com picked them up after school.

"Shouldn't you two be manning the store and booking reservations for the upcoming snow season?" Alex asked them.

They'd had an influx of rafting and camping reservations pouring in since the August issue of *Fine Tastes* came out. Com had been happy to turn people away until Vic had decided to start offering snowmobile tours. While he was glad that all their work for the family business was paying off, Alex's weekends were threatening to fill up again and he was relieved Wilson and some of their new hires had agreed to stay on for the rest of the year.

"And miss our granddaughters' big soccer game?" Commodore huffed. "No way."

As the volunteer coach for Elsa's and Audrey's team, Alex prayed for patience. "Listen, Com, you can come to the game today, but if you yell at the referee again, I'll ban you from the field myself."

"Are bats really blind?" Elsa asked, referencing the last time Commodore had been ejected from their soccer match.

Audrey whispered to Vic, who answered, "Of course we can go to Patrelli's for pizza afterward if you score another goal."

Charlotte smiled at Alex and murmured. "So much for our plans to have a quiet afternoon together."

But his fiancé couldn't fool him. Alex knew that deep down she wouldn't trade their hectic schedules and his nosy, interfering family members for the world. He brushed a loose curl behind her headband as he spoke into her ear. "If we take our own Jeep and give them enough quarters for the arcade afterward, maybe you and I can sneak away for a little hike in the woods behind our new house."

Soft pink color stole up her cheeks and she whispered back, "Don't forget to bring along our little orange tent."

* * * * *

MILLS & BOON®

Cherish™

EXPERIENCE THE ULTIMATE RUSH OF FALLING IN LOVE

A sneak peek at next month's titles...

In stores from 9th March 2017:

- **Reunited by a Baby Bombshell** – Barbara Hannay
  and **From Fortune to Family Man** – Judy Duarte
- **The Spanish Tycoon's Takeover** – Michelle Dougla
  and **Meant to Be Mine** – Marie Ferrarella

In stores from 23rd March 2017:

- **Stranded with the Secret Billionaire** – Marion Lenno
  and **The Princess Problem** – Teri Wilson
- **Miss Prim and the Maverick Millionaire** – Nina Sing
  and **Finding Our Forever** – Brenda Novak

Just can't wait?
Buy our books online before they hit the shops!
www.millsandboon.co.uk

Also available as eBooks.

MILLS & BOON®

EXCLUSIVE EXTRACT

Griffin Fletcher never imagined he'd see his
childhood sweetheart Eva Hennessey again,
but now he's eager to discover her secret—
one that will change their worlds forever!

Read on for a sneak preview of
REUNITED BY A BABY BOMBSHELL

A baby. A daughter, given up for adoption.

The stark pain in Eva's face when she'd seen their
child. His own huge feelings of isolation and loss.

If only he'd known. If only Eva had told him. He'd
deserved to know.

And what would you have done? his conscience whispered.

It was a fair enough question.

Realistically, what would he have done at the age of
eighteen? He and Eva had both been so young, scarcely
out of school, both ambitious, with all their lives ahead
of them. He hadn't been remotely ready to think about
settling down, or facing parenthood, let alone lasting
love or matrimony.

And yet he'd been hopelessly crazy about Eva, so
chances were…

Dragging in a deep breath of sea air, Griff shook his
head. It was way too late to trawl through what might
have been. There was no point in harbouring regrets.

But what about now?

How was he going to handle this new situation? Laine, a lovely daughter, living in his city, studying law. The thought that she'd been living there all this time, without his knowledge, did his head in.

And Eva, as lovely and hauntingly bewitching as ever, sent his head spinning too, sent his heart taking flight.

He'd never felt so side-swiped. So torn. One minute he wanted to turn on his heel and head straight back to Eva's motel room, to pull her into his arms and taste those enticing lips of hers. To trace the shape of her lithe, tempting body with his hands. To unleash the longing that was raging inside him, driving him crazy.

Next minute he came to his senses and knew that he should just keep on walking. Now. Walk out of the Bay. All the way back to Brisbane.

And then, heaven help him, he was wanting Eva again. Wanting her desperately.

Damn it. He was in for a very long night.

Don't miss
REUNITED BY A BABY BOMBSHELL
by Barbara Hannay

Available April 2017
www.millsandboon.co.uk